Josephine's Fortune

Serenity Inn Series

Josephine's Fortune

Kay D. Rizzo

BROADMAN
& HOLMAN
PUBLISHERS

Nashville, Tennessee

© 1999 by Kay D. Rizzo
All rights reserved
Printed in the United States of America

0-8054-1675-7

Published by Broadman & Holman Publishers, Nashville, Tennessee
Editorial Team: Vicki Crumpton, Janis Whipple, Kim Overcash
Page Design: Sam Gantt Graphic Design Group
Typesetting: PerfecType, Nashville, Tennessee

Dewey Decimal Classification: 813
Subject Heading: FICTION
Library of Congress Card Catalog Number: 98-49464

Library of Congress Cataloging-in-Publication Data
Rizzo, Kay D., 1943–
      Josephine's Fortune / Kay D. Rizzo.
            p.   cm. — (Serenity Inn series ; bk. 3)
      ISBN 0-8054-1675-7 (pbk.)
      I. Title. II. Series: Rizzo, Kay D., 1943–   Serenity Inn series.
PS3568.I836J67   1999
813'.54—dc21

                                                                98-49464
                                                                CIP

1 2 3 4 5 03 02 01 00 99

— Dedication —

To my friend Jeni Crane.
You are loved and appreciated.

~ Contents ~

Prologue

EVENING SHADOWS GATHERED IN THE NOOKS and alleyways of the Van der Mere home on Capitol Boulevard in Albany, New York. Leaves of yellow, brown, and orange swirled across the quiet boulevard, leaping and pirouetting in the brisk autumn wind. A squirrel, scampering along a branch of an elm tree beside the red brick townhouse, scolded the young woman poised behind the tall, narrow bank of leaded, bay windows.

Josephine Van der Mere's hand trembled as she reread the words written in the graceful scroll handwriting of Miss Clare Thornton, of New Orleans, Louisiana.

> Dear Mrs. Van der Mere,
>
> I am writing this letter to give you the good news that Samuel Pownell did not die in a storm off the Carolinas as reported. He is alive and, while not feeling too well at the moment, he is on the mend. Eb Greene, a compatriot of mine, found Mr. Pownell unconscious in the bayou five miles from my home. Mr. Pownell had been beaten, robbed, and left for dead by his attacker. The thief stole Mr. Pownell's identification papers

and his letters of introduction. Using the pur-loined identification, the robber made his way to Hamilton, North Carolina, where he used Mr. Pownell's identification to book passage on the *Wayfarer,* a schooner bound for the California gold fields. And as much as we have been able to piece together, the man received his comeuppance by drowning on the ill-fated voyage.

Shock gripped Josephine's heart and mind as she read the unbelievable tale.

Mr. Pownell suffered from a broken leg, damaged vocal cords, a broken arm, and several broken ribs, as well as injuries to the head that rendered him unconscious for a time. Once we discovered he'd been reported lost at sea, Mr. Pownell was most anxious to contact you and his daughter, Serenity.

Dr. Boggs, my family physician and a great man sympathetic to our cause, would not allow Mr. Pownell to communicate verbally until recently so that his throat could heal properly.

To ease Mr. Pownell's increasing anxiety, I told him I would write this letter for him. I would appreciate it if you could pass on the good news to Samuel's daughter, to his brother, to Abe, and to his solicitor, Mr. Cox. All should be cautioned against repeating the news of Mr. Pownell's con-dition to anyone as there is still some question as to whether or not the hunt is still on for him.

"I-I-I can't believe it!" Josephine gasped. "Sam's alive! He's alive!" She wanted to shout, dance, and celebrate, but shock rendered her speechless and paralyzed her limbs. Pinpoints of light danced before her eyes and she found it difficult to breathe. Feeling like a young girl twirling too long on the lawn, she grabbed the back of her rosewood rocker to steady herself, the letter quivering in her free hand. "I refuse to swoon! I refuse to swoon! I am not a frail dowager!"

A gentle knock on the door partially restored her balance. "Yes," she called, her voice heavy with emotion. "Who is it?"

She heard the voice of Annie, her personal maid. "It's me, Miss Josephine. Annie. Is something wrong? I thought I heard you cry out."

Josephine took several deep gulps of air but didn't bid Annie to enter the room. If the news about Sam had to be kept secret, Annie was the last person she should see right now. The girl was too perceptive. She would spot that something was wrong immediately. "I'm fine, dear. But could you do me a favor and find Abe? I need to see him right away in the library."

"Of course, if you're sure you'll be all right. You don't sound too good."

Josephine tried to hide the emotion in her voice. "I'm fine, honest."

"All right, if you're sure . . ."

After listening for the sound of Annie's footsteps on the stairs outside her bedroom door, Josephine returned her attention to the letter in her hand. The words swam on the paper as she reread the message. Tears dropped on the ink, creating artistic splotches on the inexpensive scrimshaw paper. She covered her face with her hands, and the tears flowed as the pages of the letter flittered to the floor.

"Sam's alive! My Sam's alive . . . ," she whispered. Hearing the words aloud triggered something in her mind. "Oh, dear God, my Sam's alive! Thank You! Thank You! My Samuel's alive!"

~ 1 ~

Shadows in
the Night

A FLURRY OF WIND AND RAIN DRIFTED ACROSS the quiet cobblestone street of the city. A tiny woman, cloaked in a brown homespun wool cape, slid to a halt at the corner of a dark alleyway. Her breath hung in the November night air as she tugged the hood of her cape closer to her face.

An unseasonably cold wind had swept down from Canada, bringing with it bone-chilling rains. The unexpected freeze would turn the leaves on the maple and elm trees to gold, red, and orange. However, the cold in Josephine's heart wasn't due to the frigid breeze sweeping about her feet but the icy fear gripping her heart. She paused to breathe a quick prayer. "You promised to keep me in perfect peace if I keep my mind stayed on Thee. I'm trying, Lord. I really am."

The candlewick of the streetlight on the corner flickered above twenty-nine-year-old Josephine Van der Mere's head. Muted shadows cast artful shapes on the brick walls and garbage-strewn cobblestones of the roadway behind her. Was her imagination playing tricks on her, or had she seen the man slip into a doorway behind her? The same man she'd spied earlier at the docks?

A shiver skittered down her spine. Senses sharpened by years of scurrying along the underbelly of the city alerted the delicate blond woman to the presence of a stranger. She first observed him lingering behind one of the boathouses at the docks. Thinking him to be a deckhand stealing a smoke, she cast an analyzing glance at him. She couldn't afford to completely ignore him, not in her line of business. A woman alone in a harsh world needed every edge she could get.

Her suspicions rose as she noted his clothing, the clothing of a land traveler, not a seaman. The black Benjamin overcoat fell midcalf on the man, revealing a pair of Wellington boots, scuffed and dulled by years of horseback riding. A well-worn black felt hat shaded his eye. Only his straight, aquiline nose could be seen above the man's dark, heavy mustache and beard.

Josephine spied the stranger a second time lingering near the neighboring slip to her barge, *The Silver Garnish*. She'd paused to scan the riverway after delivering her "cargo." A couple of fishing boats sat dry-docked for the season. An abandoned jury-rigged schooner appeared ghostly in the stormy late afternoon light. All forms of life, human or otherwise, had long since sequestered themselves elsewhere to wait out the storm. All forms, that is, except herself and the stranger who'd stepped into the lee of a stack of wooden crates when she glanced his way.

The woman wrapped her cape tightly about her body and plunged into the teeth of the storm. Up one alleyway, down the next, past an ale house, beyond the public stables, Josephine scurried, occasionally glancing over her shoulder as she ran. At the corner of Main Street and Delmar Avenue she spotted him again, this time not more than a hundred feet behind her.

Instead of heading west toward her townhouse on Capitol Boulevard, the woman hoisted her skirts and dashed across the empty intersection to the clapboard-sided inn on the opposite corner. Quickly, she slipped through the heavy oak door to safety. Once inside she lowered the hood of her cape and brushed the excess rain and sleet from her shoulders.

Conversation stopped at the corner table where four sailors sat devouring bowls of mutton stew and slices of homemade bread. A woman alone in the night? Eighteen fifty or not, all good and proper ladies would be in their parlors toasting their brocade-slippered toes before their husbands' hearths. The fact that she wasn't, in their minds, left her open to their crude and suggestive ribaldry.

The other three tables in the room sat empty. In a few hours, after the ale houses closed for the night, the inn would fill with grog-soaked sailors. The word had spread through the nautical community that one could expect clean beds at a fair price, but no hard liquor at Ben's place, the Shanty Inn.

Ignoring the sailors' leers and lecherous mutterings, Josephine made her way through the eating area and into the back room. Her simple homespun clothing camouflaged for the onlookers that the woman with the silken blond hair could be anything but a peasant woman, a chamber maid employed at the inn.

Ben, the middle-aged, rotund innkeeper, glanced up from his ledger book open on the counter before him, scowled, then closed the book and followed the young woman into the back room.

As the door slammed behind her, Josephine shivered. "Brrr! It's cold out there tonight," she said. She turned and gave Ben an apprehensive smile.

His scowl deepened. "What are you doing here? You're not supposed to be here unless there's an emergency."

Josephine's hyacinth blue eyes widened with concern. "Ben, I think I'm being followed."

"That's not good." He took a deep breath and frowned. "Do you know who it is?"

She shook her head. "I've never seen the man before today." She slipped her heavy woolen cape from her shoulders and let it slide to the glistening oak paneled floor. Warmth from the fire in the massive stone fireplace filled the room and quickly set out to replace the damp chill in her bones. "I thought I'd stay here a few minutes until he's gone."

Ben nodded. "We've been transporting too much cargo these last few weeks. You, in particular. I do have other conductors I can use, you know."

"I know."

His eyes narrowed. "It's like you have a private vendetta, Josie. You can't let it become personal, you know. It will affect your concentration."

She picked at the fibers of the rough textured cape in her hands. "And just how does one stay detached? Today I helped a pregnant seventeen-year-old runaway escape from her master, the father of her unwanted child. And it shouldn't become personal?"

"Is it because of Sam?" he asked. "All the runaway slaves you manage to transport to the next station will never bring Assemblyman Pownell back, you know."

Assemblyman Pownell. How formal the title seemed for the man Josephine loved. For a moment she remembered the day he proposed to her. She also recalled the reaction his teenage daughter, Serenity, had had to the announcement. She realized that Ben still believed that Sam, her fiancé and best friend, had been lost at sea.

How she missed him! Knowing him to be alive and recuperating in New Orleans made her heart ache to be with him instead of pretending he was dead. *But if this charade is the only way I can protect him from the bounty hunters,* she reasoned to herself, *I'll do it.*

Josephine also remembered the cause to which they'd dedicated their lives. She knew her zeal for the cause would be no less determined five or ten years in the future. Like it or not, her crusade was personal. She'd risk her entire fortune to save even one child from a life of slavery.

Ben narrowed his eyes to mere slits behind his tiny goldrimmed spectacles. "You don't think that the man following you is one of those bounty hunters you tangled with in Auburn, do you?"

"I don't know." She placed one hand over her mouth in thought, then shook her head, her brow knitted with concern. "I doubt it. Albany is a long way from the trouble at Lake Cayuga. And it's been a couple of months. Besides, those two would have trailed Sam, not me."

A violent cough erupted from the innkeeper's throat. He choked, then broke into a fit of uncontrolled coughing until he gasped for breath.

Josephine ran to his side, gently touching his heaving shoulder and his arm. "Are you all right, Ben? Can I get you a glass of water or something?"

Shaking his head, the man waved his hand, then gave a ragged wheeze as he gasped for air. "I-I-I'll be all right."

"Ben! That doesn't sound good. Maybe you should get away from this cold climate," she urged, "go where it's warm and sunny year-round."

"Me? I'll be fine. It's just a little rattle, courtesy of the queen's coal mines. It's true that on nights like this . . . You know, Josie, maybe you're the one who should get away for a while. I'm worried. Maybe you should leave the conducting to us men."

Josephine's eyes snapped; the color in her cheeks heightened. "What do you mean, leave the transporting to you men? I'm as good a conductor as any you have and you know it, probably better than some."

Her hands on her hips, she whirled about in front of the massive stone fireplace heating the dingy office. Her gray linsey-woolsey skirt swooshed about her ankles, and her creamy white gauze peasant blouse contrasted with her heightened color in her porcelain complexion. "How many of your male conductors can pass himself off as a chambermaid, I ask you? Or as a child? Or a schoolgirl? Or a—"

Ben laughed. "All right, your argument is valid. But it's a dangerous occupation, m'girl. Being female won't protect you if you get caught. For that matter, being a woman might bring you more pain. And the pay is lousy." He laughed again at his wry humor.

Josephine chuckled and seated herself on a petit-point upholstered footstool in front of the roaring fire and waved her hands before the dancing flames. "O-o-oh, that feels so good."

The man lowered his unwieldy body into the well-worn, burgundy and navy upholstered, wing-backed chair beside her. She watched him fold his meaty hands across his protruding stomach before he spoke. "I'm serious about your going away for a few days. It would give me and the boys time to find out just what your mystery man might be up to. Believe it or not, we can handle things here in Albany without you."

"I doubt that!" Josephine laughed and hunched her shoulders in delight. "I know. You all take good care of me and I appreciate it. If you hadn't been here for me after

Sam . . ." She saddened as she stared for several seconds into the flames, remembering the tragedy that had separated her from the man she loved.

"About the trip?" the man questioned.

"Huh? Excuse me, but what trip?"

The innkeeper picked up a cherrywood pipe from a pipe rack on the stand beside his chair. As he tapped it on the edge of a crystal ashtray, a mist of ashes fell into the tray. "The one you're going on tomorrow," he continued reaching for his hand-tooled leather tobacco pouch.

Josephine sighed. Though she'd never admit it, she was grateful to have someone care enough to tell her what she should do. She rose to her feet. "All right, if you think it's best for the station."

"Best for the station nothing. It's best for you, young lady. Since Samuel's death, you've buried yourself in the cause. It's time you got out and met people, and not as a chambermaid, but as the sparkling and lovely widowed socialite, Josephine Van der Mere."

"Josephine Van der Mere . . ." The woman gave an odd little chuckle. "I hardly remember her."

"It's time you got reacquainted. She's quite the lady, you know." He shifted his considerable weight forward in the chair.

A knock sounded and the door opened. A short, wiry, bowlegged man wearing a white cotton apron over his gray wool pants and shirt entered and tipped his bald head toward Josephine. "Madam." He turned toward the innkeeper and handed him a note. "Boss, a sailor brought this to the kitchen door. Said it was for you. Sure weren't for me since I can't read a word, not a word."

"Thanks, Barney," Ben mumbled as his eyes scanned the scrap of soiled paper. "Did he say anything else?"

"Nope, just told me to give it to you. He said you'd know what to do about it. Gotta' get back to my McRafferty stew before it boils down into a casserole." He chuckled at his attempt at humor. Josephine grinned in return. He again nodded toward the young woman, then he turned to leave.

"Wait," Ben called, "do you have someone out there who can escort Mrs. Van der Mere to her home?"

The cook's face brightened. "Oh, yes sir. Abe. He just came in lookin' for her."

Josephine visibly relaxed at the mention of Abe's name. Abe, the tall, commanding Negro overseer of the Pownell's Cayuga Lake estate had vowed to Samuel Pownell, his employer and friend, that he'd watch over Josephine until the assemblyman could return for her.

Once the fire-gutted estate was sold, Abe, his wife Dory, their eleven-year-old son Jonathan, and a servant girl named Annie moved east to Albany with Josephine. Abe took his job as Josephine's bodyguard seriously.

When Esther, Josephine's head housekeeper, retired and went home to Holland, Dory took over the running of the estate with an efficiency and grace that surprised even the longtime members of the household staff. Before long the couple became irreplaceable to the young widow of the former Dutch sea captain, Peter Van der Mere.

A relaxed smile crossed Josephine's face. Ben smiled back. "Wonderful!" he said. "Thanks, Barney. Tell Abe that Mrs. Van der Mere will be right out."

The cook nodded and left, closing the door behind him. The innkeeper handed the letter to Josephine. "This might interest you, Josie. Perhaps we can kill two birds with one stone. We have special cargo coming in to New York City on the ship *Vesuvia* at the end of the week—a fourteen-year-old girl." He scowled at the note. "You have friends in Manhattan, don't you? Our station there is closed for a time until the officials lose interest in it."

"You know I do." Josephine arose to her feet. "The Morlands have been begging me to visit them for months now. However, they do not know about my little involvement in the operation. Should I involve their home without their knowledge?"

Ben arched an eyebrow and shifted his head wisely.

"You would, wouldn't you?" she asked.

He smiled. "You'll have to do what you think best for you, Josie."

She frowned and paced to the other side of Ben's chair. "Jon and Geneva were friends with my late husband and with Assemblyman Pownell. For some reason, they, and you, think you must mother me." She patted the bald spot on the back of his head. "I haven't had a mother since I was a child, you darling ninny."

"Mother, smother!" the innkeeper sputtered. "Are you addlebrained or what? I ain't nobody's mother."

Josephine kissed the innkeeper's forehead. "You'd make a great mother, you old garter snake, you. And take care of the cough, you hear?" Before he could reply, she threw her cape over her shoulders, blew him a kiss good-bye, and slipped out of the office door.

"Godspeed," she heard him call as the door closed behind her.

At the reappearance of the pretty little chambermaid, the sailors resumed their taunting until out of the corners of their eyes, they spotted the massive Negro wearing a navy pea jacket and canvas pants, standing in the corner by the door. The loudest of the foursome's lower jaw dropped as the black man straightened to his full height of six feet, four inches and swaggered two steps toward them. The three others followed his terrified gaze. Suddenly all four men found their bowls of McRafferty's stew extremely fascinating.

"Bless you," Josephine whispered and smiled as she hurried to his side. "Abe, I'm so glad you came looking for me. How did you know where to find me?"

"I've been worried." The middle-aged black man held the door for her as she stepped out into the storm. "Missy, you had me going for a time. I checked the barge; no one was there, not even Capt'n Becker. The skiff was gone. Why didn't you come right home after delivering the girl?"

Josephine frowned. The last thing she wanted was another "mother" worrying over her, but like it or not, both Abe and Dory did just that. "I think I was being followed, so I thought it wise to take a detour."

The man's face darkened as he helped her into the brougham coach and signaled for the driver to take them home. "Someone followed you?" Abe climbed in and closed the door behind him. "I didn't see anyone when I came in," he confided.

She shrugged. "Well, I could be wrong, but it's hard to think three sightings coincidental."

"Not hardly. So tell me, what did the stranger look like?"

"Black. He wore all black."

"Are you saying you were followed by a Negro?" Abe asked.

"No, no. His clothes were black and his beard was heavy and black. There was something about him that I couldn't just dismiss." She jiggled her foot nervously. "Ben suggested that the stranger might be one of the bounty hunters we encountered at Sam's place last summer, but that's not likely . . . is it?"

"I doubt it. We would have noticed those guys long before now. A country bumpkin with a Southern drawl would have been detected easily."

Remembering the note she clutched in her hand, she handed it to Abe. "Ben asked me to make a run to New York City tomorrow."

"Tomorrow? That's impossible. I have a shipment in storage right now that I must deliver in the morning."

"That's all right. I thought I'd take Annie with me. We can do the switch thing since it's a young girl I'll be meeting."

"I'm not comfortable with that, especially after you told me about the mystery man. I should go with you." By the jut of his chin, Josephine knew the man had made up his mind. "And this storm. It could get much worse before it gets better."

"The snow's not sticking; it's too warm. I'll go by rail. It won't take very long at all."

"I don't know . . ." Abe looked worried. "I wish Sam were here."

"Me too." She cocked her head up toward Abe's stern face. "This isn't a matter of debate here. I am going." She added, "I appreciate everything you and precious Dory do for me, but you can't shadow my every move, you know. If anyone understands why I must do this, whatever the risk, you do."

Smiling down at her, his eyes softened. "I know. I know. Is there anything I can do?"

"Yes, if you could send a wire to the Morlands telling of my unscheduled arrival, it would be appreciated."

"All right. I'll do that first thing in the morning. I still don't like it and I'm certain Mr. Pownell would object as well."

Josephine blushed at the mention of Sam. *If only you knew how right you are,* she thought.

The carriage swayed as the horses strained to haul the heavy boxlike coach up the slippery hill to the Van der Mere townhouse. Josephine braced herself against the side wall and the seat. When her emotions once again settled, she whispered, "Thank you, Abe. I can always count on you." The woman smiled and touched his arm with her doeskin-gloved hand.

"You know, I could come with you if I sent—"

"You won't send anyone. Annie and I know what to do. We've managed it many times over the last couple of months. First, she'll slip out of the Morland's house before dawn so no one will know she's gone. Then we'll dress the runaway in Annie's clothing, and she and I will make our way to the train station under the eyes of the public. Anyone seeing us will think she's my maid."

Abe wagged his head. "I'll admit that your deceptions have worked many times before—but in Albany, not New York City. You're not familiar with the escape routes there."

"What escape routes? All I need are the directions to the railway station."

The carriage came to a stop. Abe opened the door, but paused before disembarking. "And if someone stops you? Or Annie?"

"Abe, you are a dear, dear friend and I love you." Josephine smiled tenderly into the man's concerned brown eyes. "Annie, God, and I will deal with the problems as they occur, my friend, just like always."

~2~

A Fanciful Affair

JOSEPHINE'S HEART SKIPPED A BEAT AS SHE twirled in front of the mahogany-framed, silver-backed, freestanding mirror. She gazed about at the luxurious decor of the Morland's guest room. She felt a twinge of guilt for enjoying the luxury, as much as she did. At times she had to remind herself of the poverty she'd experienced as a young child growing up in Boston. Then Captain Van der Mere came along and changed her fortune overnight.

The skirts of her rich French blue taffeta gown rustled about her ankles. After six years of marriage to her wealthy sea captain, followed by the last three as his widow, she still had trouble seeing herself as a rich matron. She felt like she was playing dress-up in her mama's closet, except she'd never known her mother.

If it hadn't been for Charity . . . . How she missed her dearly departed friend, Charity Pownell. The beautiful and vivacious wife of the New York state assemblyman had taken the young widow under her wing and taught her how to be a lady. *And if you don't open your mouth,* she told her reflection, *you may be able to pull it off at least one more time.*

Learning the finer points of society's expectations wasn't

all Charity taught her. Charity, a former Quaker, loved the arts, in particular, fine literature. She insisted that reading was a necessary part of Josephine's refinement, especially the Bible. "It is the basis of the literary greats. But more than a collection of narratives or poetry," Charity insisted, "it is God's Word to us, His children. He loves us and speaks to us through these sacred pages. Listen to this . . . ." She took the book and read from Psalm 139.

> Whither shall I go from thy spirit? or whither shall I flee from thy presence? If I ascend up into heaven, thou art there: if I make my bed in hell, behold, thou art there. If I take the wings of the morning, and dwell in the uttermost parts of the sea; Even there shall thy hand lead me, and thy right hand shall hold me.

"How beautiful!" Josephine whispered, allowing the exquisite word pictures to fill her imagination.

"But, as lovely as it is, it's more than beautiful poetry, Josephine. It's a promise, don't you see? Our Creator Father promises that wherever we go, He will be with us." She flipped quickly through several pages to the back of the book. "Another place, in the book of Hebrews, says, 'I will never leave you nor forsake you.' Never! You know how you always say you're alone in the world? You're not ever alone."

And now, less than a year after Charity's death, Josephine turned and gazed at the treasured gift from her friend resting on a library table in front of the Belgium lace-covered window. How she missed the delightful times she and Charity had spent together studying the promises in that book. A whisper of guilt washed through her as she recalled falling in love with and becoming engaged to her best friend's husband after Charity's death. *I don't deserve his love*, she told herself. *His daughter Serenity was right, even if she did change her mind about me later. I'm certainly not worthy to walk in dear Charity's shoes.*

"Miss Josephine? Miss Josephine?" Annie, Josephine's personal maid, called again. "Miss Josephine. Did you want me to press your other taffeta crinoline?"

"Uh, I'm sorry. What did you say?"

"I wondered if you wanted me to press another petticoat or will those you have on be enough?" The sixteen-year-old girl with the latte-brown skin and the burn-scarred hands stood to one side of the mirror holding the crinoline in question.

Josephine glanced at her own reflection in the mirror, swooshing first one way, then another. "I'm not sure. What do you think?" The gown of morning-glory blue French taffeta with its bevy of crisp petticoats felt luxuriously delicious against her silk hose and blue satin, spool-heeled slippers. That the blue in Josephine's eyes perfectly matched the blue of her gown didn't go unnoticed either. Dressing up always lifted her spirits. For a moment, she could almost forget the tragedies that had dogged her life in recent months. "Tell me what you think," she asked again.

"You are beautiful, Miss Josephine, utterly beautiful," Annie cooed. "You will set New York City's high society afire tonight."

"But what about the extra crinoline? Do I need it?"

"You're perfect just as you are," the maid's eyes sparkled with delight.

"I think I need a little glitter, don't you?" Josephine opened a red velvet satchel lying on the end of the golden silk plissé spread covering the massive four-poster mahogany bed. She took a diamond droplet earring from the pouch and held it up to her left ear. "What do you think?" she asked, brushing aside her golden curls for a better view. "And of course, the matching necklace."

"Beautiful." The younger woman's eyes misted. "They were always my favorites."

Josephine glanced quickly toward her friend and lady's maid. "I know." Slowly the blond woman placed the earring back in the pouch. "Maybe I shouldn't—"

"No! No! Mr. Pownell gave them to you to wear and to enjoy. You know Miss Charity would want you to wear them as well."

"I would send them to Serenity if I could be certain they would reach her. They need to be hers, since they were her mother's."

Josephine recognized the look of loneliness in Annie's eyes at the mention of Charity and her daughter, Serenity. Charity had rescued Annie from a life of slavery and had given her a home. The two little girls grew up together, wearing similar gingham and chambray dresses, cared for by the same nanny, and studying with the same tutor. After the fire, the girls parted; Annie to the East to Albany, New York, and Josephine and Serenity heading west with Reverend Cunard and his family to Independence, Missouri.

The occasional letter from Serenity didn't do much to ease either of their loss. Both women's eyes swam with tears. Josephine dropped the earring back into the velvet pouch. "Maybe it's too soon. Oh, I wish I hadn't allowed myself to be talked into this party tonight. I'm not ready. I'm likely to burst into tears over my hostess's famous bouillabaisse!"

Annie giggled. The servant girl couldn't suppress her buoyant nature for long. Even after her hands were terribly burned in the house fire at the Pownell estate on Lake

Cayuga, she would find something humorous to say through her tears. The doctors in Albany did what they could to ease the girl's pain, but it had been a long recovery. Only recently could Annie pick up tiny objects with her fingers.

Determining to follow the girl's lead, Josephine clicked her tongue and made a face at herself in the mirror. "I believe Geneva Morland could convince a sea captain to purchase a shank's mare."

The younger woman giggled, then declared, "You'll have a lovely time at Mrs. Morland's little waltz tonight. Wear the earrings and necklace. I know Miss Charity would want you to," Annie coaxed, gazing admiringly at the glint of the diamond pendant peeking out of the red velvet. "They're so lovely."

The servant girl arose to her feet in one gracious gesture. "Shall I style your hair now?"

"Yes, please. . . ." Josephine reached for a linen hankie lying on the bed beside the pouch and dabbed at her eyes. "Should I wear my silver combs?" The woman piled her tousled golden curls loosely on her head. "Shall we gather the curls in a cascade down my back or should I catch it all up in combs?"

Annie, her eyes sparkling with pleasure, picked up the tortoiseshell hairbrush and began brushing Josephine's silken locks.

"Like spun gold," she often said as she counted out the strokes. Styling Josephine's hair was her favorite task.

"What if I catch it all up with your silver combs . . ." She took a handful of Josephine's hair and gathered it atop the woman's head. ". . . and leave one long curl dangling down the side of your face, like so?"

"Hmm, I think I like that. Let's try it." Catching a glimpse of Annie's scarred, disfigured hands in the mirror, Josephine saddened again.

During the months following the terrible fire at the Pownell's lakeside home, every day had been excruciatingly painful for the young servant girl. For a time the doctors feared they might need to amputate one of her hands. But slowly, painfully, Annie's hands healed, thanks also to the healing power of Dory's herbal concoctions and her prayers. Dory, Josephine thought, was another great addition to her home.

Not only was Dory the best head housekeeper she'd ever had, but the woman was a bastion of strength to Josephine, especially after she received the news that Sam was lost at sea. Dory had become the spiritual lifeline for Josephine that she'd lost when Charity Pownell died in the carriage accident. Although Josephine had given Annie and Abe's family a place to live after the fire, they'd given her much more.

"I will never leave you, nor forsake you. . . ." She'd lost so many people she loved—Charity, her best friend and confidant; then Sam, her newly acquired fiancé; and last, Serenity, their daughter, when she moved west. Yet, along the way, God had brought others into her life to help her cope with her losses. Josephine absently gazed into the mirror as Annie tucked and pinned the glistening tumble of curls into place.

"Do you still think about and miss Miss Charity often?" Josephine asked.

Annie smiled slowly. "Almost every day. Missus was so good to me. She insisted I learn how to read, you know."

"Me too," Josephine admitted. "I was an ignorant child of the streets, and Charity taught me how to deal with my situation—first to read, then how to be an elegant 'lady' like she was. High society would have eaten me for dinner if it hadn't been for her."

Annie nodded, her mouth filled with hairpins as she worked.

"And my being one-eighth Negro didn't bother her in the slightest. On the contrary, it bound us together in a common cause."

Annie eyed her mistress in the mirror. "I still can't believe it. I've never seen anyone 'cross over' as well as you."

"Sometimes I feel guilty for denying my race."

The maid shook her head. "Quite the contrary. You couldn't do half of what you do for our people if the world knew you weren't totally white, especially those in high society. You can make a difference for all of us."

"Thanks." Josephine smiled. "You are very kind. Sometimes I'm not sure I'm making that much of an impact."

When Annie pinned the last of Josephine's curls into place, Josephine removed the droplet earrings from the pouch and attached them to her earlobes. The little maid helped her fasten the necklace as well. Josephine smiled at her reflection. "So, do I look ready to tame a few tigers?"

"More than ready." Annie giggled at her mistress's metaphor. She was glad that she'd only have to help serve the strange little appetizers. Mrs. Morland had asked Josephine if Annie would be willing to help the staff with the serving that evening. At first Josephine demurred, but Annie assured both women that she'd be more than happy to help. "It will give me something to do, and I'll get to enjoy the party while doing it."

"As long as you're comfortable with it," Josephine cautioned.

The butterflies in Josephine's stomach subsided after she whispered a quick prayer for peace "in the midst of a storm." *Why should I be nervous? I've attended these things dozens of times in the past,* she argued with herself. *If it weren't for Geneva, my hostess, I wouldn't consider attending. And I'm not looking for a husband! If only she knew. . . . If only everyone knew.*

Her first reaction upon receiving the shocking letter from a lady in New Orleans was elation. Sam was alive. He hadn't drowned in the shipwreck as had been reported. Instead the man who stole his money, the man who beat him and left him for dead, was the one who drowned aboard ship. *Talk about delicious irony,* she thought.

The letter arrived in late September. Since the shipwreck, Sam had been cared for by an old maid schoolteacher. With a broken arm, a broken leg, and a concussion, it had taken a few weeks before Sam could let anyone know he was alive.

"Believe it or not, I'm a celebrity of sorts," the second letter said. "There are those who would like to use my capture as an example to others in the Underground Railroad. Can you believe it?" he wrote. "Until I get on my feet, it might be wise not to let my existence become common knowledge. But I believe Clare explained that to you in the first letter. I don't know how far-reaching my enemies' influence might be."

And so Josephine abided by his wishes. Only Abe had been told; even Dory, Abe's wife, did not know Sam was alive. She'd written Sam's daughter, Serenity, living in Missouri, but hadn't heard from her yet. Josephine was beginning to wonder if her letter had been lost.

Sam knew that Josephine's first reaction would be to go to him. So he asked her to wait until spring, when traveling would be a lot safer in the Northern states at least. As the days passed, however, it was becoming more and more difficult for her to obey his wishes.

Josephine kept the treasured letter in the back fly of her Bible. She picked up the Bible and hugged it to her chest. She did this whenever she felt lonely or had to face a trying situation. She smiled to herself. Here she was attending a party where the hostess would try to "match" her up with some eligible young swain, and Josephine's real purpose would not be to meet a man, but to spirit a young runaway north to safety.

Orchestral music drifted up the winding staircase from the Morland's glittering ballroom. Josephine squirted herself with a spritz of exotic perfume imported from the Orient. She placed the crystal perfume bottle on the dressing table and breathed deeply. *This is it.*

Catching the skirt of her taffeta gown with one hand and the mahogany railing with the other, she pasted a smile on her face and descended the elegant marble and mahogany staircase.

"Ah, our guest of honor," her host called at her appearance, "the lovely sprite of a woman, Mrs. Josephine Van der Mere."

Josephine smiled up in the face of Jon Morland, her late husband's friend and business partner. She took his hand and allowed him to introduce her to a gaggle of businessmen congregated in the Morland's impressive marble-tiled foyer.

After the death of Peter Van der Mere, Jon Morland had sold the fleet of ships they'd partnered and gone into the export/import business. A country as young as America clamored for European and Eastern goods. And in return, the Old World hungered after the New World's cotton, wheat, and corn. Among the leading wheelers and dealers in the state, if not in the country, Jon Morland hobnobbed with the highest of New York's social and political society. That's how he came to meet and befriend Assemblyman and Mrs. Pownell.

Before Charity Pownell's death, the Morlands and the Pownells often included Peter Van der Mere's widow in their social plans. The three women, Geneva, Charity, and Josephine, spent hours together, attending all the obligatory teas, lawn parties, and other midday events. Feared and tolerated by many of the social set, the three women gave "voice" to the consciences of other members of New York's upper crust. Charity had attended the women's conference in Seneca Falls, New York, and returned on fire for the cause of women's suffrage. As for Josephine, her focus remained with her people. And Geneva had moved on to the newest cause *du jour.*

It had been the same with Geneva's interest in spiritual things. While Charity's devout commitment to her God spread to Josephine, Geneva wasn't equally impressed, at least not until Charity's death. Now, Josephine realized, Geneva was asking questions, searching for a purpose to her friend's life and death.

As Josephine passed through the aromas of expensive perfumes and imported cigars, nodding and smiling as she walked, her eyes darted from one full beard to the next as if expecting to see Sam. *He's not here, you ninny. Stop it. Get a hold of yourself.* As she scolded herself, she felt an arm slip into hers and heard her hostess whisper, "Relax! Enjoy yourself."

Josephine turned to her friend. Between gritted teeth, she said, "I'm trying. This is what you call a 'little' party?"

Geneva shrugged and grinned sheepishly. "The guest list got out of hand. Everyone wanted to greet you, darling. You've become a legend in these parts."

"A what?"

"A legend. We've all heard about the way you flim-flammed those two bounty hunters." Geneva chortled. "Imagine! Turning flour sacks into babies!"

"How did you—"

Her hostess nodded wisely. "You'd be surprised at how much I know about yours and the assemblyman's exploits."

"B-b-but-I-I-I—"

"Oh, don't worry. We're all proud of you for daring to do more than talk about your beliefs. I am embarrassed to say, I would never have the courage to do what you and Sam did."

Josephine smiled. "I've discovered one does what one must under the circumstances."

"See? That's why you're so noble and I'm such a coward. I'd turn tail and run in the face of a lynching mob, not stand up to them like you did."

Josephine blushed. "Believe me, you would come through for Jon if it were a matter of life or death."

"Perhaps. But for tonight, all you and I need to do is relax and enjoy ourselves. Here, let me introduce you to our guests. Mr. Flendheim," Geneva called to a portly gentleman standing next to the pianoforte. "I would like to introduce you to my dear, dear friend, Josephine Van der Mere." To Josephine, she said, "Mr. Flendheim is a shipping magnate from South Africa, if you can imagine such a thing. He's an avid boar hunter." In a conspiratorial whisper, Geneva added, "Pigs! Wild pigs!"

Josephine smiled graciously at the middle-aged man who was obviously new on the New York scene since Peter, her first husband, died. She extended her hand and dipped her head, "Mr. Flendheim, how very nice to meet you."

The man took her slender hand in his chubby one and touched his lips to the back of her fingers. "I am honored to meet you, madam. I've heard great things about your late husband."

"Thank you, sir." She tipped her head and smiled. "Our hostess tells me you are from Southern Africa and that you enjoy boar hunting. Just what is boar hunting?"

It didn't take long for Josephine to regret her insightful question. The man was a fountain of information on boars—sizes, coloring, behavior. *Everything I never wanted to know,* Josephine chuckled to herself. *The man's a bore on boars.*

Guests continued to arrive, some she recognized and others she did not. Whenever she thought to escape from Mr. Flendheim, he'd take her arm and draw her closer to him. When her host finally rescued her from the man's grasp, Josephine had the wildest urge to plant a grateful kiss on Jon's white bewhiskered cheek.

Jon eased her into the clutches of yet another guest, Hans Folsonburg, junior ambassador from Norway. The ambassador's eyes brightened at the sight of the diminutive blond woman with the dazzling blue eyes and radiant smile. Tall, blond, and speaking with an affected English accent, the young man determined to impress Josephine with his feats of valor. While her mind wandered about the crowded ballroom, she knew she didn't need to worry Mr. Folsonburg might notice.

Gazing abstractly at the vibrant colors in her hostess's paisley draperies, Josephine was startled to feel an arm encircle her waist and hear a familiar voice speak in her left ear.

"Well, well, imagine seeing you again after all these years, Mrs. . . . er . . . Van der Mere, isn't it? You are far lovelier than I remembered."

Slowly Josephine glanced over her shoulder. Her eyes widened in an instant of fear and distrust when she recognized an all-too-familiar face from her past. A dark-haired man of medium height and striking good looks grinned possessively down at her. "Bradley? Bradley Williams. What ever are you doing here?"

"I should be asking you that, my dear. The last I heard you were roughing it in the wilds of New York State with some rabble-rousing politician." His sardonic smile still rankled her.

Her eyes narrowed and her nostrils flared in anger. "Auburn is hardly the wilds of anything and Assemblyman Pownell certainly is not a—"

The man threw his hands up in defense. "Hey, hey, hey! You still can't take a bit of joshing, can you? You always were a serious little puss, but never so elegant. Look at you, a real lady now. I always knew you were a diamond in the rough."

The junior ambassador tried to break into the conversation, but Bradley Williams skillfully maneuvered himself and Josephine away from him. Josephine glanced over Bradley's shoulder and saw Hans Folsonburg shrug and turn away.

She returned her attention to the problem at hand. *How dare anyone slander a man like Sam! You aren't even worthy to fetch his pipe!* Like always, Charity Pownell's wise counsel echoed through her mind, "A soft answer turneth away wrath. . . ."

Try as she might, Josephine couldn't contain all her ire. Her left eyebrow arched defiantly as she smiled up into

Bradley's face. "Why, thank you, kind sir, for your extravagant compliments." Her droll tone wasn't lost on the brash interloper. She glanced down at the unwanted hand resting on her waist. "If you would be so kind as to unhand me, sir. . . ."

Bradley Williams chuckled aloud and slipped his offending hand into his coat pocket. "Is that any way to treat the man who almost—"

"Almost, Mr. Williams, never won a foot race or the hand of a lady."

"Lady . . . ," he chuckled. "Ah, Josephine, my dear, I know you so well." He took his pinkie finger and intertwined it in the blond ringlet dangling along the left side of her face. "I know about the tiny birthmark hidden away so exquisitely behind your ear. I know—"

"If you will excuse me, sir—" Her gaze turned to steel. She stepped back.

When she turned to walk away, he grabbed her elbow. "Oh, no, I'm not finished—"

"Indeed you are, sir!" Josephine hissed through clenched teeth, removing his hand from her arm.

"Bradley, old chap," a male voice interrupted from across the room. Josephine followed Bradley's gaze in the direction of the voice. She studied the face of an average height, sandy blond-haired man as he made his way through the crowd toward them. There was something disturbingly familiar about him. For a moment she forgot the pesky man standing by her side. Had she ever met the stranger before? Josephine couldn't make the connection.

"Oh? Peter! There's someone here I want you to meet. Remember how I was telling you about the lovely Mrs. Van der Mere?" Bradley slipped his arm possessively about Josephine's waist. She struggled to escape without making a scene, but he held her fast. Taking one of her hands, Bradley held it out toward the approaching man. "Be polite, my dear." Bradley growled. "You're a lady now, not an alley kitten like you once were."

She shot a look of hate at Bradley. "If you don't unhand me immediately—"

The young man with the sandy blond hair and reddish mustache took Josephine's hand before she could declare her actions should Bradley refuse to accede to her wishes.

"Mrs. Van der Mere! What a pleasure!" He kissed her fingertips and continued holding her hand far beyond the respectable time. "I have heard so much about you, more than you can imagine."

Squirming herself out of Bradley's grasp, she scowled. "Sir, do I know you? I'm afraid you have an advantage over me. Mr. Williams failed to introduce us properly. What is your name again?"

The young man grinned toward Bradley, then back at Josephine. "Peter is the name, Peter Van der Mere, the third." He bowed from the waist. "At your service, madam."

Josephine gasped. "Excuse me?" Color drained from her face as she studied the young man's fine features. She'd heard her deceased husband speak of his son who was about her age. "After his mother died, I sent him to live with his aunt in Holland, hoping she could do for him what I'd failed to do. He's a total wastrel. I gave him his inheritance and washed my hands of him."

Josephine remembered how cruel her husband's words had sounded. When their union failed to produce children, she wondered about the banished heir to the Van der Mere fortune. On his death bed, Peter had warned, "No money.

Give my son no money. He's had his share and wasted it on loose women and elderberry wine."

She stared at the young man and shook her head. "You're Peter?"

"That's right, madam. Or should I call you Mama? I'm your late husband's son. The one he banished to Europe so he could marry his pretty little guttersnipe." Peter Van der Mere's eyes glinted with devilish cruelty.

-3-

A Stranger
Comes Calling

 STUNNED, JOSEPHINE SHOT A QUICK GLANCE
at Bradley. Bradley widened his eyes in an
affected question and shrugged as if Van der
Mere's announcement was news to him. In
the background, the woman could hear the sound of swooshing skirts as the guests shifted to the dance floor. She recognized the popular Strauss waltz the orchestra was playing, but
she couldn't take her gaze from the face of the young man
who'd introduced himself as her husband's only son.

Her face softened. She reached out and touched the
young man's cheek. "Of course, I can see a strong resem-
blance to your father." She gave a nervous chuckle. "His
eyes, you have his deep blue eyes. . . ."

Peter eyed Josephine critically as her eye misted with
tears. "Please, Mrs. Van der Mere, don't embarrass both of
us with an unnecessary display of emotion. It's not as if you
loved him or anything."

She felt a stab of pain. "I loved your father very much.
He was kind and generous and lonely."

"And his money spends well, doesn't it?" Peter sneered.
"I know about you, Mrs. Van der Mere. My friend, Bradley
Williams, told me all about you."

"And just what did Mr. Williams have to say?" Josephine glanced at Bradley, her former fiancé, the Harvard man her mother wanted her to marry so badly. What could he say that would bring such a look of scorn to her stepson's face?

Directing her gaze to Peter's solemn face, she urged, "Peter, you and I need to talk other than in the middle of Mrs. Morland's party. I want to hear all about your travels and about your aunt."

Peter's eyes narrowed even further. "I agree."

She hastened on. "Are you in the country long? Will you be coming to Albany while you're here? You know you're always welcome in your father's house."

A tap on the shoulder caused her to look in the face of Mr. Flendheim. "Madam," he said, "could I have this dance?"

She smiled, then looked questioningly at Peter.

"Go ahead. We can talk later, Mrs. Van der Mere." Her stepson smiled magnanimously.

She gave Mr. Flendheim her hand and waltzed away on his arm.

Josephine's lovely figure decorated the arm of several men that evening until she begged off and asked her current partner for a sip of punch. He'd barely left her side when Annie slipped up behind her.

"Here," Annie whispered, "a note. He's waiting at the kitchen door for instructions."

Josephine slipped the note into the edge of her glove and smiled. "How are you doing?"

Annie brightened. "I'm tired but it's fun serving at such a sparkling party. Don't the ladies look lovely in their silks and satins? I especially like that dark blue velvet one. Isn't it magnificent?"

Josephine nodded, her smile intact. "Come with me." Before her last dance partner returned with the refreshment, she and Annie slipped through a set of double doors leading from the party room.

The two women found themselves in Jon Morland's study. Two stories of books lined three of the room's walls. A fire crackled in the massive stone fireplace on the fourth wall. Several brass candlesticks and matching wall sconces shed light on the deep tones of rosewood furniture and the muted tones of a large carpet from the Middle East.

"Should we be in here?" Annie whispered.

For a moment, Josephine leaned her back against the closed doors and took a deep breath. "It's all right," Josephine glanced about the empty library. Removing the note from her glove, she unfolded the paper and held it under the light from the nearest candle to read.

"Need to deliver cargo tonight. Law on trail. Recommend transfer of cargo as soon as possible."

Upon reading the note, Josephine held it to the flame and watched as the fire slowly began to devour it. "Annie, tell the waiting gentleman that tonight is fine; as is tomorrow."

"Do you want the cargo delivered here?"

"Yes."

A frown swept across Annie's face. "But the party guests? And the Morlands?"

"Exactly. With so many people coming and going, one more will hardly be noticed. Give the gentleman my burgundy velvet cape for the girl to wear. Bring her in through the kitchen and up the back stairs to our room."

Annie smiled and gave a shallow curtsy. Her voice held a note of caution. "Yes, ma'am."

Earlier Geneva had looked questioningly at Josephine when Josephine told her she wanted Annie to sleep in her room. "I'll feel better to have her there should I waken in the night," Josephine had said. "Unfamiliar surroundings and all, you know." Geneva seemed to buy the explanation.

Without warning the double doors behind the two women burst open—Bradley Williams and Peter Van der Mere III stepped into the room.

"Josephine, my dear, we looked everywhere for you. We thought you'd left the party early," Bradley said, strutting into the room, his thumbs tucked into the waist of his pants. His eyes flashed from the ashes of the burned note to Josephine's sudden flush of color. "Are we interrupting something?"

"Yes, are we interrupting something?" Peter echoed. "When you left, the party lost its glamour for me."

"Me too," Bradley added. While the two men's voices sounded light and charming, their eyes scanned the room, missing nothing.

"It's so nice of you to say," Josephine responded. She touched her forehead with the back of her fingers. "And no, you were not interrupting a thing. I was merely sending my personal maid on a mission of mercy. I'm afraid I get a little heady spinning across the floor to Strauss' beautiful music."

"You aren't feeling well, my dear?" Bradley asked, moving in as close to Josephine as he dared.

"Nothing serious. I'm sure I'll be fine in a few minutes." Josephine cast him one of her practiced "society" smiles, then turned to Annie. "Go, my dear, and ask the cook if she has any Vichy water from Saratoga left. The bubbles always help when I become lightheaded."

"Perhaps a glass of wine would work faster?" Bradley whispered close to her ear, as Annie left to find the cook. "Wine is an incredible cure for most anything that ails you."

A moment of panic rose in Josephine's heart. She could feel undertones of malevolence in the man. She sensed he was dangerous, and that she should beware. She'd learned at an early age to read people, to listen to her senses whenever they warned her of danger. They'd never misguided her.

Brushing past him with as much grace as possible, Josephine scooted around a large library desk. She picked up a thin pamphlet laying on the corner of the desk and began fanning herself. "Ooh, that feels so good. It's a little warm in here, don't you think? Thank you anyway, Mr. Van der Mere, but an alcoholic drink is the last thing I need tonight, I assure you."

"So you still don't drink spirits?" Bradley asked incredulously. "I would have thought by now you would have acquired a little more polish, considering the high falutin' circles you've crashed—"

"Crashed? The only party crasher I know is Mr. Van der Mere here. At least, I didn't see your name on my hostess's guest list." Out of the corner of her eye, Josephine spotted a remaining corner of the note she'd tried to destroy. It had fallen onto the candle brioche. She gingerly slipped the unburned scrap of the note from the base of the candle into her glove. She flashed Bradley another smile and moved away from the candelabra. "And you, Mr. Williams, your silver tongue never fails you, does it? In or out of the courtroom."

Bradley grinned the first natural grin she'd seen for the evening. "And your sharp tongue hasn't dulled with time, either, my dear."

Impatience underscored Peter's voice as he interrupted Josephine and Bradley's banter. "If I stop by the Morland's tomorrow, say for afternoon tea, will you and I be able to have that little chat you mentioned earlier?"

Josephine remembered the runaway who, at that very moment, was being spirited into the house and upstairs to her room. It would be imperative to get her north of New York City as soon as possible. Every moment she was in the Morland house the girl was in danger of being discovered. "Oh, I'm so sorry, Peter, but I'm leaving for Albany first thing on the morrow. I have business to attend that cannot be held off any longer."

"Business with my father's money," he mumbled as he turned his face away from hers.

"Excuse me?" she cooed, batting her eyelashes in innocence. "I missed your last remark, Peter. It must be the orchestra music beyond these doors. They do seem to be playing louder than they did earlier in the evening."

Peter glared but did not repeat himself. Seeing the tension growing between Josephine and his uninvited guest, Bradley broke in. "I've watched you blossom over the years, Josephine, from a scrappy little guttersnipe to a beautiful and accomplished young lady. If I'd known you had such potential to dazzle, I never would have listened to my mother and broken our engagement."

"More's the good fortune of us both. And alas, the bad fortune for Mrs. Williams—your wife, not your mother." She arched her eyebrow and slowly edged her way toward the door.

"Oh, dear Josephine, I'm injured to the quick! There is no Mrs. Bradley Williams, I fear. No one could measure up to you." The young lawyer maneuvered his way closer to her. Josephine inched further to her right. He pursued until he'd cornered her between himself and a bank of books.

He lifted his arm, blocking her escape. She tried to duck under the arm, but he closed the gap, making her escape impossible. A beautiful woman, she'd experienced her share of mashers, but mostly, she lived in a polite society that maintained a modicum of courtesy and respect for women. Her heart pounded with a fear she'd never before felt. If she screamed, it was a good chance no one would hear her above the orchestra's music. And if they did hear her, her name would be scandalized along with the two cads in the room. *Annie, come back*, she breathed. *Oh, dear God, send Annie back!*

"You always did try to run away from my kisses, didn't you? That was one reason I asked you to marry me, you know—you were always so reluctant. Were you reluctant with Captain Van der Mere? Or with Assemblyman Pownell? Maybe you're a black widow, you kill the men you love?"

She shot a quick glance at the door, less than three feet from where she stood. One good lunge and she'd step back into the crowded ballroom, free of her predators. She shot a pleading glance at Peter. Instead, he stepped in front of the closed doors, barring her only exit. Surprisingly, however, he did come to her rescue. "Leave her alone, Bradley. There are plenty of willing ladies around."

Bradley stepped back, releasing Josephine from her terrifying cage.

Peter moved toward her, his face hard and cynical. "Perhaps we can talk now?" he said.

Choosing to take the offensive, she strode past him to the door. "This is neither the time nor the place, as I said previously, Mr. Van der Mere." She reached around him for the doorknob. "Now, if you would excuse me?"

The man gave a chuckle, then pressed his hand against the door. "You know, I'd like to see that air of arrogance wiped off your face, Mrs. Van der Mere. Bradley, come over here—"

A knock sounded at the door. "Mrs. Van der Mere? Mrs. Van der Mere! Open the door. Let me in," Annie called. "I can't open the door. It's stuck."

Josephine started to speak, but Peter shushed her.

"She won't go away, you know," Josephine warned. "Annie will bring on the king's guard before she'll walk away from trouble."

Beyond the door, they could hear Annie shouting above the music. "Mr. Morland, the library door is stuck and poor Mrs. Van der Mere is trapped inside!"

Peter and Bradley exchanged glances, then Peter released the pressure on the door.

"My goodness!" Peter exclaimed to the startled host and little personal maid. "I do believe the door was stuck. A good carpenter can take care of the problem for you." The two men strolled out of the library without further comment.

Annie rushed to Josephine's side. "Are you all right, Miss?"

Blanched and shaking, Josephine hugged her maid. "Thanks to you, I am. And to you, Jon."

The older man who'd been such a friend through the loss of her husband, and more recently the loss of Sam, gathered her into his arms. "Are you sure you're all right? You look pale as a ghost, my dear." To Annie he said, "Go and fetch Geneva. Your mistress looks ready to pass out."

"I-I-I'm fine, Jon." Josephine took a deep breath and

brushed a few sweaty strands of hair from her forehead. "Did you know that Peter's son would be here tonight?"

"Peter? Peter Van der Mere? That was Peter's boy? Why, no. He wasn't on the guest list. I would never have recognized him."

"I believe Bradley Williams invited him."

The man nodded. "Ah, yes, the young lawyer from Boston. Dear Geneva invited Mr. Williams to supply the single ladies with available males for dancing, I'm sure. But Peter?" He glanced around the edge of the door, searching the crowd for a glimpse of the two young men. "No, I didn't know Peter was back in the United States. What did he want? Was he bothering you?"

"He wants to talk. I suspect about his father's estate. My husband warned me about giving him any more money. Peter gave him his share of the inheritance and sent him off to Europe."

"Yes," Jon admitted. "The boy was in and out of trouble. He was sent to his aunt's in Amsterdam hoping a few years on the continent would straighten him out."

"I'm afraid it didn't help." She shook her head sadly and smoothed her gloved hand over the satiny finish of an occasional chair. "He spent his money, then sent for more, which Peter refused to give him."

"What are you going to do?"

"I don't know. My first instincts are to give him whatever he wants. Peter was his father, after all." She looked up into her friend's eyes. "But I will probably have to respect my late husband's wishes since he spelled them out quite plainly in his will."

Geneva burst into the library like a thunderclap. "Oh, my dear Josephine! Whatever is happening? Are you all right? Annie came and told me those horrid young men were abusing you. Is that right?"

"I am fine, dear, just fine."

Jon turned toward his wife, his brow knitted with concern. "Did you know that the Williams fellow brought along a friend tonight?"

The woman blushed and fluttered nervously. "Well, yes, but he assured me the man would be one of quality, one that would blend in with our other guests."

She looked at her husband, then at Josephine. "I'm so sorry, but I did so need extra eligible men."

Josephine placed her hand on her hostess's arm. "It's all right. You had no way of knowing what those two had in mind. I know Bradley Williams can be very devious."

Jon cocked his head to one side. "How did you say you knew Mr. Williams, if you don't mind?"

"Not at all," Josephine assured him. "My mother worked as a housekeeper in Boston for Bradley's socialite mother. When I reached my teens, I would help in the kitchen. I'm a pretty good cook, if I say so myself." Her face relaxed into a grin. "I met Bradley during his Christmas recess from Harvard. We fell in love, or at least, what I thought was love. When he asked his mother to allow us to marry, he set off a firing cannon in the household."

Geneva slipped her arm around her husband's waist. "I know how that can be, you being from a different class and all. Did she send you away?"

"Not before she had a friend of hers check into my mother's past and uncover the fact that my mother was the granddaughter of a South Carolina plantation owner and a young slave girl. Needless to say, even Bradley didn't want to muddy the pure Williams' bloodline."

Geneva stared at Josephine in surprise. "I don't believe it! Your blond hair; your blue eyes; your porcelain white skin; and your delicate features . . . Incredible! You're an octoroon!"

Josephine tilted her chin defiantly. "I do hope my being an eighth Negro doesn't offend you."

"Of course not! But I must ask, did your husband know? Knowing Peter . . ."

Josephine shook her head sadly. "No, I never told him. I was still shaken from losing Bradley when I met Peter. Peter and I only knew each other for three weeks before we married. I'm sure he never suspected."

"Remarkable!" Geneva commented again. "Now I can understand why you and Charity became entangled with the campaign to free the Southern slaves, her being a former Quaker and all. I could never understand your passion. But aren't you afraid your secret will be made public?"

Josephine frowned, pausing to consider her answer carefully. "Yes and no. I'm not ashamed of who I am, thanks to Charity. She made me see that I am a child of God and that's what's ultimately important. And being able to pass into the white society has been a definite advantage, I admit." Her frown deepened. "My life has been much easier than my black sisters."

"But doesn't the Bible say God cursed one of Noah's sons and that's where the Negroid race came from?" Geneva asked. When she heard her words, her face reddened. "I'm sorry."

"Don't apologize. I used to think that too until Charity introduced me to a loving God, a bigger God than One of revenge and punishment."

"You don't believe God punishes humans for their sins?" Jon asked, his voice rent with surprise.

"Of course, God chastens those He loves, isn't that what Scripture says? But I don't believe He planned for any child of His to enslave any other of His children. According to the New Testament, we are all free in Christ, regardless of our skin color or our native language."

Jon shook his head in wonder. "If that really is Christ's teaching, it's phenomenal. It's revolutionary." He glanced over his shoulder toward the next room. Dancers in sparkling colors glided past the open library doors. Occasionally someone would glance toward the darkened library as they waltzed by.

"I'd like to hear more," Jon admitted, "but right now Geneva and I must get back to our other guests."

Geneva placed her hand on Josephine's forearm. "Will you be all right, my dear?"

Josephine smiled. "I'll be perfectly fine, thank you. I do think I'll slip up to my room, if that's all right?"

"Oh, please, yes. Go right ahead. We'll make your apologies to anyone who asks. Won't we, Jon?" Geneva glanced up at her husband.

"Of course. For that matter, instead of exiting through the ballroom, take my hidden staircase up to our bedroom." He walked to the other side of the library and touched a lever beneath the fireplace's marble mantle. "It comes out in our bedroom at the top of the stairs." The highly polished wood panel slid open revealing the narrow staircase. "Go ahead now." Josephine thanked them and hurried across the room.

"Would you like me to have your maid prepare a pot of chamomile tea for you to help you sleep?" Geneva volunteered, always eager to please.

Josephine glanced over her shoulder at her hostess and smiled. "That would be very nice, thank you."

As the panel slid closed behind her, Josephine found herself engulfed in darkness. Carefully she felt her way up the staircase. The smell of dust and mothballs filled her nostrils. When she reached the landing, she could smell the aroma of Geneva's French perfume and she knew she was safe. Josephine pushed open the door.

She paused in the narrow doorway to get her bearings. *The foot of the bed is opposite the double doors,* she told herself. *There should be a freestanding mirror to my right, or am I on the other side of the bed?* She felt around in the darkness until she made contact with one of the posts of the massive walnut canopy bed. She took a step forward in the darkness. That's when she heard a tiny gasp come from beneath the bed.

"Who's there?" Josephine hissed. She waited and listened, but only silence followed. She ran her hand along the length of the bed to guide her in the darkness. Josephine carefully crossed the open space between the foot of the bed and the double doors leading into the hallway.

Bam! She smacked her toe into a door. She felt around for the knob, then opened the door. Josephine sighed with relief when candlelight from the mirrored sconces flooded into the room from the hallway. Closing the door behind her, Josephine hurried down the hallway to her room.

Expecting her room to be dark as well, she picked up a single candelabra from an Italian marble-topped table as she passed. When she opened the door, she found Annie folding Josephine's nightgown.

The girl straightened, her eyes wide with fear. "Oh, you startled me!"

"Sorry. Mrs. Morland is looking for you to ask you to bring me . . ." Josephine glanced about the room. Her dresses and petticoats lay scattered about like on wash day;

her underclothing draped half in and half out of partially open bureau drawers. "What happened in here?"

"I-I-I don't know." Annie flailed her hands about nervously. "I came up from the kitchen to prepare your bed and I found the place ramshackled."

Josephine bent down to retrieve her tortoiseshell hairbrush from the Persian carpet, then placed both the brush and the candelabra on the nearby dresser. "Did you see anyone come up here during the evening?"

"Not a soul. Worse yet, I sent the cargo up here just minutes before I found this mess." Annie clutched Josephine's night dress to her chest. "What if they found her in here and took her away? I looked in the trunk and she's not there."

Josephine smiled. "I think I may know where our little runaway is," she said as she walked out of the room into the hallway. "She probably heard someone coming and hid in the closest room possible."

Picking up the candelabra, Josephine led Annie down the hall and into their hosts' bedroom. She carefully lifted the end of the imported slubbed silk bedspread to find two dark and terribly frightened eyes peering up at them.

-4-
Before the
Dawn

 VIOLA MAE CHESTERFIELD FLED A LARGE
cotton plantation in Georgia after her owner
sold her fiancé to a neighboring plantation.
"I couldn't stay any longer. The night the
massa' throwed a birthday party for his boy, everyone got
drunk. So's I ran'd away," she said. "I know'd nobody be
missin' me until late the next afternoon, being Sunday-go-
to-meetin' and all."

Josephine smiled at the wisdom sparkling in the young
woman's eyes. The moment she'd seen the girl peering out
from under Geneva's bedspread she knew that the girl
couldn't be more then fourteen or fifteen. Coaxing her out
from under the bed and into the guest room had been a
chore. The young girl didn't trust people with white faces.

Josephine gazed at the girl with admiration. *This child
has made it through swamps, across swollen rivers, through
dense forests—hundreds of miles—alone.*

"I followed the drinkin' gourd nights and slept days. I
heard the darkies sing while workin' the fields. Nobody talks
'bout it, but everyone knows." Every slave in America knew
about the "drinkin' gourd." The drinkin' gourd was a name
for the Big Dipper constellation. The north star of the

constellation directed fugitive slaves to freedom in Canada.

"One night I got tree'd by a pack of huntin' dogs," Viola Mae continued, "but I jumped from a limb into a river before the bounty hunters show'd up. I swam upstream 'til they lost my scent." Her eyes glistened with determination as she gazed into Josephine's face. "Ma'am, I ain't goin' back. Please don't make me go back."

"How did you find your way here?" Josephine asked.

"A Negro preacher found me tryin' to cross his property a week ago. He let me hide in his barn until an old black woman in his congregation could bring me to the city and to Corky, the nice man who dropped me off last night. Corky said it would be risky because this house is not on the route."

"He's right. Mr. and Mrs. Morland are not part of the underground system." Josephine paced to the bay windows and back, her hands clasped behind her back, her brow coursed with concern. "I understood you were coming by ship?"

"No, ma'am. That must be somebody else."

Josephine pressed her fingers against her forehead. *If this girl is right, there's another runaway out there that didn't make her connection.* "We could be in danger," she said. "First thing in the morning we have to get you out of here!"

"I ain't goin' back. I swear on my pappy's grave, I ain't goin' back!" Viola Mae's voice held a note of resolution far beyond her years and her station in life.

The young matron smiled tenderly. In her eyes, Josephine could see her own grandmother's resolve. The girl gazed at Josephine's flaxen blond hair and deep blue eyes. The ebony-skinned girl reached out to touch the woman's porcelain white face, but, within inches of Josephine's skin, withdrew her hand quickly. "But you're one of 'em. I ain't never seed one of 'em help a darkie like me."

"There are a lot of caring people who will help you. And I'm not sending you back, Viola Mae. Don't worry. Annie and I will deliver you to the next station. And before you know it, you'll be in Canada and free! There will be others to help you, and some of them will be white-skinned like me. Now, let me explain how we will transport you to Albany." She turned toward Annie, who'd been busily packing Josephine's clothing in a large hump-backed, leather-bound trunk with brass fittings. "But first, tell me, how did you happen to end up in the Morland's bedroom?"

The girl glanced toward Annie, then back at Josephine. "I climbed the kitchen stairs just like Annie said. At the top of the stairs, I heard someone coming up behind me. I got scared and I ran into the first bedroom I found."

Josephine scowled. "Did you see who followed you?"

"No, ma'am. It was a man, I know'd that. After I closed the door, I don't know what happened next."

I'll bet I know what happened next. Josephine smiled rue-fully. *He ransacked my room, that's what happened.* "Annie, you were in the kitchen; did you see anyone?"

"No. He could have slipped by me while I was outside the kitchen door talking with the conductor."

"You spoke with the conductor?" Josephine shot her an anxious glance. "Annie! Did anyone see you talking with the conductor?"

"No, but if they had, they'd just think Corky was deliv-ering food supplies."

"At such a late hour?" Josephine shook her head. "I don't like it. Why did you take such a risk?"

Annie dipped her head. "I don't know, ma'am, except he had the nicest smile and I . . . I'm sorry."

Josephine strode to the bay windows overlooking the Morland's courtyard. "Annie, you can't allow yourself to become distracted like that. It could mean your life some-day." She wrapped her arms about herself. "I hate to think of what might happen to you if you aren't on alert at all times."

"Yes, ma'am." Annie's eyes swam with tears. "He was so . . . nice and well . . ." She blushed and swiped away her tears with her hand. "I wish I were as smart as you."

Josephine broke into a smile. "Do you know I once said that very same thing to Charity Pownell? And I'm going to tell you the same thing she told me, Annie. You're smart enough, but you must become wise. And wisdom, as you know, comes from God."

"I don't know . . ." Annie nibbled on her lower lip. The runaway slave watched the interplay between the two women. They treated one another as equals, even though one was black and the other white; one was a servant and the other her mistress.

Josephine crossed the short distance between Viola Mae and Annie, then wrapped her arms around Annie's slender shoulders. "Annie, am I pushing you too fast? Are you sure you're up to this mission?"

Annie nodded. "I'll be all right, I promise. I won't let such a thing happen again."

"I love you, you know that don't you?" Josephine squeezed her as if the threat of losing her was imminent. "I'd hate to have anything bad happen to you because of me and my mission."

"Your mission?" Annie looked at the woman in surprise.

"It's my mission too. Remember, it was Mrs. Pownell who rescued me from the life of a field hand."

"You're right, my dear. How arrogant of me to think this cause rises and falls on my performance or devotion." She took a deep breath. "It takes hundreds of caring people to run the Underground Railroad effectively, each one doing his or her own part. If only I could remember that."

"Oh, by the way, did this conductor of yours mention anything about the young girl we came for, the one coming in by ship?"

"He isn't my conductor, Miss Josephine." Annie blushed. "But, no, Corky didn't say anything about any other fugitive coming in."

"Hmm, I hope nothing bad happened to her. Maybe we should offer up a short prayer for her, wherever she may be."

Josephine and Annie bowed their heads and closed their eyes. "Dear Father, somewhere between New York City and Alabama there is a frightened girl who needs You. Protect her. Renew her strength and her faith. Help her obtain the freedom she deserves, if it is in Your plan for her life. Amen."

Josephine crossed the room and opened the door to the hallway. "It sounds like the party is breaking up. We need to get Viola Mae safely hidden before our hostess checks to see that I'm all right."

Josephine scooped up a handful of her clothing that had been strewn across the floor. "Annie, help me stuff all this into the trunk. Viola, you'd better hide under the bed until Geneva leaves. Annie, when our hostess comes into the room, keep your face turned from her. The less chance she can recognize you later, the better."

Annie scurried around the room collecting the odds and ends of clothing still to be packed, as Viola Mae scooted under the bed for cover. "Oh, Viola, you will be my personal maid tomorrow morning. You will need to avoid being recognized as well." Josephine lifted the edge of the jacquard woven bedspread and peered beneath into the runaway's frightened eyes.

"I'll do my best, ma'am," the girl assured her.

"Good. That's all I ask. Mainly, don't speak to anyone unless you're spoken to."

The girl grinned. "Oh, I can do that, I reckon."

"Good." Josephine straightened and smoothed the bed coverlet. Picking up her Bible, she opened it to the starched, ecru crocheted cross bookmark—her first attempt at crocheting—she'd placed in Isaiah 25. She read the verses aloud while Annie finished the packing. "O Lord, thou art my God; I will exalt thee, I will praise thy name; for thou hast done wonderful things; thy counsels of old are faithfulness and truth. . . ."

She'd just finished reading the chapter and the first two verses of chapter 26—"Thou wilt keep him in perfect peace, whose mind is stayed on thee: because he trusteth in thee"—when she heard a knock on her bedroom door. She and Annie looked at each other with fear evident in their eyes. Josephine closed her eyes, breathed a quick prayer and called, "Yes? Who is it?"

"It's Geneva, Josephine."

Josephine hurried to open the door. "Yes, what is it?" She pretended to hide a yawn behind her hand.

"Er, Jon asked me to, er, ask you to join him in the library. He has business to discuss with you. He says it's important."

"Of course. Just let me slip into my shoes." She lifted the skirts of her ball dress to reveal her stocking-clad feet. The worry in her friend's eyes disturbed her. *If she knew . . .* Josephine shot a guilty glance toward the bed skirt. *It's not to be helped,* she reasoned with herself. *There are more important issues at stake here.*

Josephine entered the library and gazed about the room. Only a wisp of smoke trailing from Jon's ivory and ebony pipe was visible behind the massive hunter green leather wing-backed chair as the man sat staring into the crackling fire. She glanced at the ashes scattered about beneath the candelabra where she'd burned the note earlier. The dark-toned Persian rug muffled her steps as she crossed the room to where her longtime friend sat.

"Jon? Geneva said you wanted to see me? About business?" For several seconds she waited for him to reply.

"Please sit down, Josephine." Without turning to face her, he gestured toward the matching leather chair across from him.

She seated herself in the large brass-buttoned chair. Her feet dangled above the floor like a child's. The man's face remained hidden from her view by the chair's upholstered wings. The entire atmosphere made her feel defensive and vulnerable. She didn't like it.

"Josephine, I asked you here without Geneva present for a reason."

"What is it, Jon?"

"Tonight, learning about your heritage put the last piece of the puzzle into place. When I heard about Sam's involvement with the band of hooligans and law breakers calling themselves the Underground Railroad, I couldn't figure out how such an intelligent man, a member of the state assembly, could allow himself to get involved in such risky and illegal practices. Now I understand."

"Jon . . ." She leaned forward. How she yearned to tell these friends of Sam that he was alive and living in Louisiana, but she knew better. "That's not true. His work with runaways began long before I met him and Charity."

"Charity? Did she know about this?"

"Yes, she was very active in the program, both raising funds and supplying shelter for the runaways. She and I first met at a fundraiser."

"I can't believe it—breaking the law right under our noses! Sam, I wasn't surprised at, but I credited Charity with more sense than that." The man growled. "I loved Sam as a brother, but I love the law more." He turned to face Josephine. "When the state assembly censured Sam for the fiasco out there near Auburn, I agreed with their decision."

Josephine studied her hands for several seconds rather than look at her old friend.

"I care deeply for you as well, Josephine," he continued.

Josephine reddened. "I-I-I'm glad."

"Like a daughter . . ." Jon narrowed his gaze as he studied Josephine's troubled face. "Truman, my head butler, reported to me that a young runaway was delivered to my house tonight during the party. He says that your maid is involved. I believe he even searched your room." He cleared his throat. "At first I wanted to believe that your girl was acting outside your knowledge, but after observing her and you, I no longer believe she acted alone."

He waited for Josephine to answer, but she gazed into the flames of the fireplace. "Josephine, are you harboring a fugitive in my home without my knowledge?"

Josephine, for all her usual cleverness and skills at

deflecting suspicion, sat speechless. She'd always wondered how she'd feel and how she'd answer if ever questioned. Would she lie? Evade the truth? Or what? If it were someone else asking the questions, someone she didn't respect or love, maybe she would. But it wasn't her life at stake. She would not be the one to be dragged south in chains, subjected to all kinds of indecencies for her disobedience. *Do I have the right to be honest at Viola Mae's expense?*

"In all your ways acknowledge Him and He shall bring it to pass." The familiar words ran through Josephine's mind as she stared into the burning coals. She could almost hear Charity's sotto voice reciting the text.

Lifting her eyes to meet his, the young woman replied, "Yes, sir, I am. Viola Mae is in my room with Annie as we speak. She's a fourteen-year-old field worker who ran away after her master sold her beau to a neighboring plantation. Though she hasn't told me, I suspect that her sweetheart has run away as well and that they plan to meet when they reach Canada." She took a deep breath. *There! I've done it,* she told herself as she watched her friend digest the troubling secret she'd just revealed.

"You've placed Geneva and me in a awkward position, Josephine."

"I know. And I'm sorry."

"Sorry? Sorry for breaking the law under my own roof?"

She dropped her head. "I'm sorry. There's more, I'm afraid. Viola Mae isn't the runaway we came for. It seems she was funneled into the system by a farmer in Pennsylvania. We don't know what happened to the girl we were sent to help."

"Oh, dear God, no!" Jon rose to his feet and strode to the massive marble fireplace. He took several moments to refill his pipe with tobacco from a decorative alabaster vase. "This is awkward, awkward indeed! You might have brought the law down on our heads, Josephine. How could you? If your husband Peter knew about your foolish antics—" Suddenly, he whirled about to face her. "Do you really think you can change the system by breaking the law? Do you believe you can make a difference in these people's lives by risking your own?"

"Yes, I can, one runaway at a time." She lifted her jaw defiantly. For the first time since she entered the room she was filled with confidence. "I feel for this little girl. It was a Pennsylvania farmer who risked everything to rescue my great-grandmother and her infant daughter from a slave trader's lash. One man caring for one young mother and her child and I am here to tell about it."

"But you, you can pass for a white in any society. You've proven that here in my own house. Why do you risk detection by getting involved in such nefarious activities?"

Easing herself from the chair, she strode over to her friend, her skirts rustling in the room's heavy silence. She placed a hand on his arm and gazed solemnly up into his face. "It's because I can pass for white, as you put it, that I have an even greater obligation to assist those who can't. Don't you see?"

He gazed down at her tiny petal-white hand, then back into her wide blue eyes. "You are making it very difficult for me, my dear."

"I-I-I'm sorry," she confessed, withdrawing her hand. "You are right. What I am doing is against the law. And it was wrong of me to involve you and Geneva. I know that now. What are you going to do?"

Jon's shoulders slumped forward. He placed an elbow

on the mantle and rested his forehead in one hand. "I don't know, my dear. I really don't know. If Geneva knew about your runaway being in the house, she'd become hysterical and do something foolish."

Josephine knew Jon was right about Geneva. The woman was known to dissolve into tears when a female guest arrived at one of her dinner parties without an escort.

Jon lifted his head. His jaw hardened. He tapped his pipe against the marble mantle. "I'm tempted to send Truman for the constable. That's what I'm tempted to do."

"If you think that's best, Jon . . . ," Josephine mumbled, praying that God would somehow change his mind and his spirit. She waited and prayed while an ornate grandfather's clock in the corner by the windows gonged twelve times.

As the last gong faded on the night air, Jon placed his pipe in its ebony holder. "It's late. I think it's time we both got some sleep. We can deal with this in the morning." He ran his tongue along the inside of his jaw. "Actually, I have business at my office first thing in the morning, probably before you arise." He gazed deep into her eyes as he spoke.

Josephine's heart skipped a beat. "Really, sir?"

He continued. "I'm not sure I'll be home in time to see you off. . . ." His words trailed into the shadows.

It took a second for his words to register. But when they did, Josephine broke into a wide grin. "Oh . . ." She rushed to him and threw her arms around his neck. "Oh, thank you, Jon. Thank you. You won't be sorry. I promise you. You won't regret it."

"I didn't do anything, Josephine." He grimaced, shook her off, and stepped back to look at her. "And what do you mean I won't regret it? I'm already regretting it. Your illegal activities change everything between us, don't you see?" He pressed a hand against his temple and sighed. "I feel as if I've lost a daughter tonight."

Josephine's eyes filled with tears as she watched her dear friend agonize with his conscience, but she said nothing.

"Every choice we make, good or bad, has consequences, my dear." His shoulders sagged as he blew out the candles in the candelabra on the library table. "Consequences . . . I am sorry for those consequences." He turned, then strode from the library.

Josephine listened to his steps echo on the marble floor in the vestibule and up the stairs. She waited until she heard the door of the master bedroom close behind him, then sank into the nearest chair. Light from the dying embers in the fireplace cast a glow about the room.

Josephine's heart ached. Jon, more than any man she'd ever known, represented to her the image of a loving father. She'd never met her real father. Her husband, Peter, had been a sort of father to her, taking her from the streets of Boston into his mansion as his wife. But for the most part, she'd had to care for him as a nurse for three of the six years of their marriage. And Sam? The type of relationship between them would remain to be seen. A familiar thought niggled at her brain. *Just how old is this old maid school-teacher? Maybe she's the reason he didn't want me to come to him immediately.* Josephine and Sam's romance had been so short lived, too short to build a deep trust between them.

For several minutes Josephine listened to the rhythm of silence as could only be found in a well-stocked library. The smell of musty paper, dust, printer's ink—she'd come to love these aromas after meeting Charity and Sam. The wisdom of the ages written in the books surrounding her failed to bring peace to her restless spirit. She stared into the fire until the coals in the fireplace turned to ashes. Slowly, painfully, she made her way up the stairs to her bedroom, perchance to catch a few minutes of sleep before the new day dawned.

~5~

A New Day

THE NEXT MORNING JOSEPHINE AND HER
entourage exited the Morland house in a
flurry of hugs, kisses, and Godspeeds. The
Morland's carriage driver, outfitted in a
dark blue livery uniform with gold braid on his sleeves
and shoulders, stood proudly beside the family's shiny
maroon brougham carriage in front of the three-story, red
brick townhouse when the Morland's houseboy carried
the travelers' luggage to the curb. The driver and the boy
hoisted the heavy humpbacked trunk into the carriage
bonnet, then loaded Josephine's smaller pieces of luggage
on top. With dramatic flair, he buffed the gold crest on
the carriage door with his sleeve, then paused, waiting to
help the wealthy young widow and her personal maid to
board.

The driver opened the carriage door for the maid while
Josephine and the lady of the house said their good-byes.
Geneva tentatively took Josephine's tiny hands in hers,
while avoiding gazing in the younger woman's eyes. "It was
smart of you to send your second trunk on ahead earlier this
morning. You are such a bright little thing, my dear. You
will come back to see us soon, won't you?"

The woman didn't give Josephine time to reply. "I am truly sorry those two odious young men gave you such a difficult time last night. See if either of them ever get an invitation to one of my social events again! Imagine! And Mr. Williams being from Boston. I would have thought better of him and his upbringing!"

"It's all right, Geneva. Don't give it a thought," Josephine assured her.

Ponderous clouds hung heavy above the city skyline. The houses and street merged in a delicate watercolor of grays, rust red, and brown. The older woman slipped her arm into the crook of Josephine's arm and strolled toward the waiting carriage. "Just what did happen in the library anyway? And what did you and Jon talk about? Whatever it was, he had a hard time sleeping afterward."

A stiff breeze from the Hudson River ruffled the hood of Josephine's gray velvet cape as she strode toward the carriage with her hostess. "Ask Jon. I'm sure he'll share his concerns with you. And don't worry; if invited, I will visit again, I promise."

Geneva's lower lip quivered. "I hope so. Jon didn't hesitate to escort Mr. Williams and Mr. Van der Mere from the premises, not before they voiced their tawdry allegations. I have to admit that, at first, I was disconcerted learning that Negroid blood flows in your veins . . . ," she whispered conspiratorially into Josephine's ear. ". . . but I'd watch out for the likes of those two if I were you. They're out to cause you trouble."

"I know. And I appreciate yours and Jon's friendship. But, Geneva, I do mean it, if my being an octoroon or my behavior brings you any embarrassment, I will stay away," Josephine assured her hostess.

"Oh, no! I should say not. I mean, well, we do have friends who, if they knew, er, well, it would be embarrassing for you and them, I fear." The woman nervously twisted and untwisted a linen handkerchief in her hands. "But me, personally? No, of course not. Why Daisy, my housekeeper, is a dear friend and she's black as the ace of spades. Ooh, I mean . . ."

Josephine smiled sadly.

"Did the assemblyman know of your, er, mixed heritage?" Geneva asked, her eyes filled with concern and worry.

Josephine laughed. "Oh, yes, both Sam and Charity knew. After Peter died, I stopped trying to hide my heritage."

"Oh. Well . . . Jon thinks . . . er, I . . . I don't know what I think." The woman knitted her brow. "I'm in a quandary. My heart tells me you are the friend you've always been. But my emotions?" She scrunched up her face. "Oh, I don't know how I feel. I've never dealt with people of color before—socially, that is."

The woman paced to the edge of the front steps, then turned to face Josephine. "The world is changing so fast that I can barely keep up. One day you think you know your friend, and the next . . . Oh . . ." She caught herself. "I'm so sorry. I didn't mean . . ."

"It's all right. I've known all my life. Though my mother had aquiline features similar to mine, she told me about my heritage when I was quite young. And for the most part, I've used the knowledge to my advantage."

"Advantage?" Geneva gasped. "How can anything so tragic be an advantage?"

"As Charity often said, 'God uses imperfect vessels to distribute the healing oil of His love to others.' What more can I ask than to be used of God, no matter how 'imperfect' a vessel I might be?"

"Imperfect?" The woman paused and studied Josephine's form and face for several seconds before she replied. "I've never met a more perfectly formed creature than you. I've often told Jon that if I had a daughter, I would want her to look just like you."

A chuckle erupted from Josephine. "Then either you or Jon would have to have mixed blood running through your veins as well."

This thought unnerved the older woman further. Josephine hurried to reassure her. "It's all right. I was just joshing you, Geneva."

The woman dabbed at her eyes with her handkerchief. "I feel terrible about this. If only I didn't know. If only I hadn't invited those two rapscallions to my party. Why'd they have to go and spoil everything?"

Josephine grew sad as she looked at her friend's troubled face. She knew that, regardless of the woman's protest to the contrary, Josephine Van der Mere would not be a guest in the Morland's home again anytime soon. Quietly, without stir or debate, she had been placed on the back page of Geneva's social calendar. How could Geneva risk New York's society discovering that she hobnobbed with "coloreds"? And she was quite certain Jon wouldn't mention her involvement with the Underground Railroad to his all-too-chatty wife. Would Geneva pass on her newest tidbit of gossip? Either Josephine's bloodline would be the main course at Geneva's next dinner party or Geneva would be too embarrassed to tell anyone of the connection. If the news got out, would Geneva pretend ignorance?

Josephine kissed the woman on the cheek, then stepped aboard the carriage. "We'll keep in touch," she called as the driver closed the carriage door behind her and climbed up into his seat in front of the cab.

"Oh, stop, Conrad, stop." Geneva flagged the driver. Josephine held her breath a moment, then leaned out the carriage window.

When she glanced out of the cab to discover the reason for Geneva's call, Josephine thought she saw a movement at the corner of the block. She shot a frightened look, first at the spot where she'd seen the sudden movement, then at Geneva. *Could it be?* She shook away the idea. *You are becoming much too paranoid, Mrs. Van der Mere!"*

Her hostess bustled to the carriage window. "Josephine dear, I forgot to tell your maid how much I appreciated her help last night. It's Annie, isn't it?"

Josephine nodded apprehensively, being certain to block her hostess's view of the servant.

Geneva continued, trying to see beyond Josephine's form to where the young black woman cowered in the seat. "The cook said the girl was a charm to work with. You trained her well."

"Thank you. I am glad she could help." Josephine smiled and took a deep breath. *Let's get out of here. . . .* "Thank you again, Geneva, for everything. Give my love to Jon. Tell him good-bye for me. Driver," she called. "We'd better be going if we don't want to miss the morning train."

Immediately the driver clicked the whip over the heads of the sturdy set of matching Cleveland Bays. The horses snorted billows of steam in the cold morning air and strained at the weight of the carriage. The vehicle edged forward and Josephine breathed freely once more.

The hood of her cape slipped from her head as she waved her last wave, then leaned back against the soft supple leather seat. "Ah, the worst is over, I think," she said as she closed her eyes and pinched the bridge of her nose to ease a headache forming behind her eyes. "I wonder how Annie is doing?"

Visions of the night before and the wee hours before dawn played again in her mind. Josephine had barely laid her head on the soft goose-down pillow before it was time to set the plan into motion.

Before the houseboy headed to the farmer's markets to purchase the groceries for the cook, before the kitchen staff began baking the day's bread supply, before the horses in the stables awoke from their night of slumber and the stable boys stirred from their cots, Annie, dressed in a maid's gray and white uniform and carrying a large paisley carpetbag, slipped out of the Morland's home and silently made her way down the alleyway behind the townhouses, across the foot bridge, through the silent city to the train station.

At least that was the plan, thought Josephine. With Annie's ticket purchased earlier, the young woman was to tell the conductor of the Albany train that her mistress had sent her on ahead to ready the traveling compartment for her arrival. Then, when no one was watching, Annie would wait in the compartment until passengers began arriving, then she would make her way to the baggage car. Once there, Annie would climb into the larger, empty trunk they'd sent on ahead from the Morland's that morning. There she would hide until she was safe at home at the Van der Mere's townhouse.

Sending Annie ahead was, for Josephine, the most frightening part of their plan. Both women knew that anything could happen to a young black girl traveling alone. She carried papers proving that she was a freed slave, but over-eager bounty hunters could just destroy such papers and take her prisoner. Once they reached a slave state, they could sell her to the highest bidder. To them, a bounty is a bounty and one Negro is as good as another. Worse, if they had an inkling that Annie might be aiding runaways, they wouldn't hesitate to beat her into submission before transporting her south to a life of bondage. Josephine brushed these frightening thoughts aside and allowed the rhythmic jouncing of the carriage over the cobblestone street to lull her into a gentle slumber.

None of them had slept much during the night as they prepared for their departure by the light of a brass candelabra. After the luggage stood ready to be transported down the stairs and Annie was prepared to leave, Josephine opened her Bible and began to read the promises of Psalm 91 as Charity had taught her to do. The words soothed her troubled soul. And she hoped they would bring peace to Annie and to Viola Mae as well.

"He that dwelleth in the secret place of the most High shall abide in the shadow of the Almighty. . . ."

Annie and the runaway slave girl listened respectfully as Josephine's lilting soprano voice read the words aloud. Peace settled on the three women—couching, comforting, cosseting their fears for the day ahead.

". . . He shall call upon me and I will answer him; I will be with him in trouble; I will deliver him, and honor him. With long life will I satisfy him, and show him my salvation." Gently she drew the crocheted bookmark in place, closed the book, and dropped it in the portmanteau she would be carrying.

"Come," she said, gesturing for the two younger girls to slip into her arms. "Let's ask our Father for His protection today."

Annie slipped quite naturally into Josephine's arms but Viola Mae hesitated a moment. She'd never embraced a white woman before, nor been embraced by one. Most white women she knew didn't want her to touch them, accidentally or not.

"It's all right, Viola Mae. We're just going to pray," Annie encouraged, holding out her hand to the frightened girl. "We start every single day this way."

Fearfully, the runaway inched over to the two women, preferring Annie's arm around her to that of Josephine's.

The prayer was short and their request was to the point. "Father, watch over dear Annie today. Give her the wisdom of Solomon. Be with Viola and me as well. May we all safely see the lights of home this evening."

Josephine kissed Annie's forehead, adjusted the hood of Annie's cape about her face, warned her to be careful, and Annie disappeared. Josephine listened as the girl descended the kitchen stairs and the back door closed.

Josephine released her breath and walked to the window. She couldn't see the young girl on the street below, but she hadn't expected to. Annie's route would be via dark alleyways and shadowed side streets.

"Viola, take Annie's bed. You and I might as well catch a few minutes sleep. We don't leave for another two hours."

As Josephine turned from the window, a movement at the end of the block caught her eye. *What?* She studied the spot where she'd seen the movement for some time. *Must have been a stray dog,* she argued as she climbed onto the overstuffed mattress and pulled the sheets up around her shoulders. *Just a stray dog . . .*

***

They boarded the train safely. Annie stayed in the traveling compartment with Viola Mae and Josephine until the last stop before the Albany station, then she and Josephine made their way to the baggage car. While Josephine distracted the porter, Annie slipped into the empty trunk and closed the lid on herself.

Once certain Annie was secure, Josephine made her way back to the compartment where Viola Mae waited. It wasn't long before the whistle sounded and the conductor made his way through the train's corridor announcing the Albany station.

The train pulled into the station amid a flurry of billowing steam and resonating whistles. As the passengers disembarked from the train at Albany, no one noticed a very ordinary looking man with a full black mustache and dressed in black trousers, hat, and matching greatcoat slip from the train and disappear into the ornately decorated depot, no one except Josephine Van der Mere. An icy chill traveled the length of her spine, for she'd seen him before—several times.

A frown coursed her brow for a moment, then she returned her attention to the luggage being unloaded from the baggage car. She greeted Abe with a wave. "Over here, Abe," she called. "Take this one first."

A look of concern passed between them. "Yes, ma'am. And how was your excursion to New York?"

"Eventful. Truly eventful." Turning to her personal maid, she added, "Annie, did you remember to bring my portmanteau?"

"Yes, ma'am." The dark-skinned young woman in the heavy wool cape nodded, her eyes round and filled with fear.

Abe hoisted the larger, heavier trunk onto his shoulders

and placed it carefully into the bonnet of the Van der Mere carriage. He stashed the rest of the luggage, helped the women into the carriage, then climbed into the driver's seat.

Within minutes, Josephine was safely home and preparing to bask in the hot bath the staff had drawn and ready for her. With Annie safe and Viola being mothered by Dory, Josephine had time to think about the bizarre weekend she'd spent at the Morlands. What kind of a coincidence was it to meet up with her ex-fiancé and the man who claimed to be her stepson? She knitted her brow and shook her head. *Peter can't be much more than a year or two younger than I,* she thought. *I can hardly blame him for being upset at his father for leaving the family fortune to a woman like me.* Josephine knew she'd not heard the last of the angry young man from Europe.

And the man in black? Where does he fit into all of this? Or does he? Idly, she unbuttoned the train of perfectly formed pearl buttons running down the bodice of her gray pinstriped traveling frock. Accustomed to the assistance of a personal maid, Josephine struggled to escape her limp, soot-stained clothing. She tossed her buckram-lined crinolines and chemise onto a pink and lavender flowered chintz lounge chair her husband had imported from Italy. She then eased her tired, aching body into the hot sudsy water filling the shiny copper bathing tub.

As fast and efficient as train travel is over ship or carriage, I'm still exhausted from the six-hour trip. She uttered a sigh of pleasure, closed her eyes, and slithered deeper into the water. The soothing aroma of rose petals and lilacs engulfed her senses. *I vow on all the spices of India, I'll never leave home again.*

The woman let her mind run through a field of black-eyed Susans and wild carrot blossoms adjacent to her childhood home in Cambridge, Massachusetts. A slip of a girl of ten ran with a butterfly net in hand, her waist-length, blond hair billowing behind her, loose and free. Josephine smiled to herself. She never could bring herself to kill the butterfly. Once she caught the delicately winged creature, she always set it free. In the distance she heard the town clock gonging off the hour and the neighborhood blacksmith pounding out horseshoes in his shop at the edge of the field.

Bam! Bam! Bam! "Miss Josephine! Miss Josephine!"

Josephine popped awake, splashing bubbles and water into her face and eyes. *What? What? Where am I?* Her field of black-eyed Susans and butterflies evaporated into the gold moiré wallpaper of her bathing room and Dory's strident voice.

Bam! Bam! Bam! "Miss Josephine! You have a guest downstairs, a young man who insists on seeing you immediately, regardless of the hour," Dory called through the closed door. "I put him in the drawing room. Should I send him away?"

"Huh? Who is it?" Josephine scooted up out of her watery cocoon.

"He calls himself Peter Van der Mere. He claims he's your stepson."

"Did you leave him alone in the drawing room?"

"No, ma'am. I left him with Abe!" The woman's firm tone brought a smile to Josephine's face. Josephine could imagine poor Peter's reaction to the fearsome and intimidating glare from faithful Abe. Josephine always felt safe around the gentle, fiercely loyal giant. The six-foot four-inch Abe could glower down the most frightening of foes.

"Dory, please see that Mr. Van der Mere is made

comfortable. A cup of tea and some of your gingersnaps would be nice," Josephine suggested as she slipped into her chemise and tightened the laces on her corset. "I'll be down in no time at all."

Dory clicked her tongue as she picked up Josephine's wet towel from the floor. "I don't much like that young man, Miss Josephine. And I don't mind telling you so. He has shifty, watery blue eyes. I wouldn't trust 'em."

"Now, Dory, you just met the man," Josephine clucked. Deciding to forego her stockings, she slipped her feet into a pair of satin slippers, then dropped two plissé crinolines over her head and tied the drawstrings at her waist. "Please, Dory, treat Mr. Van der Mere kindly?"

"Hmmph! You need to ask? When have I not treated one of your guests with respect?" The woman's full round face was devoid of emotion.

Josephine arched her eyebrow knowingly. "I remember how you treated the sheriff at Sam's place."

"Er, well . . . And I wasn't wrong either, was I?" Having leveled her parting shot, Dory exited Josephine's room. "By the way, Abe delivered the girl to Ben just before dark."

"Good," Josephine mumbled to an empty room. "By now the poor little thing is probably asleep in Ben's attic until the next conductor picks her up after midnight."

The woman searched through her wardrobe until she found a soft pink woolen dress with a matching shawl. "This will do just fine for greeting Mr. Peter Van der Mere," she muttered, removing the dress from the hanger and lowering the frock over her head and arms. She tugged at the row of whale bone buttons until she'd fastened each one up the front of the dress.

Pulling her hair into a roll at the nape of her neck, she

fastened it into place with her favorite carved ivory combs. She turned first one direction, then the opposite, in front of the mirror. *Yes, everything seems to be in place.* She placed her hands on her hips. *Ready or not, here I go.*

Josephine took a deep breath to muster her courage, then made her way down the carpeted staircase, crossed the foyer, and paused in front of the open door leading into the drawing room. As she passed Abe leaving the drawing room, the trusted servant arched one eyebrow and shook his head.

~6~

An Unexpected Guest

JOSEPHINE SMILED AT THE SIGHT OF HER husband's only offspring standing in the room his father had loved so much. Every detail of the room had been overseen by Peter Van der Mere, the retired ship captain. He'd sailed the seven seas and returned with exquisite treasures from all over the world.

The young man looked decidedly like his father, she admitted. She could see her late husband in the boy's quirky smile, his sun-streaked hair, in the tilt of his head, even in the slight stoop of his shoulders. But that's where the likeness ended. All the noble traits she'd loved about her husband were missing: the uncompromising glint of honesty visible in her husband's face, the kindness in his smile, and the humor evident in his eyes—they weren't a part of the next generation's makeup.

Josephine watched Peter Van der Mere wander about the room, examining one expensive trinket then another, turning each of them over to read the stamp on the bottom. He lingered a moment over a slim volume of Dryden poetry autographed by the English author. He ran his fingers along the glossy surface of the rosewood sofa table, then ambled to the fireplace where he gazed for several seconds at a giant oil painting of his father hanging over the mantle.

Josephine smiled, remembering how cantankerous Peter had been about having his portrait made. She'd insisted and eventually wore him down. Every time she saw the painting she was again thankful she'd persisted. The artist was scheduled to paint her portrait as well, but Peter contracted consumption and died. Josephine, grieving over her loss, canceled the contract. *Why would I want a painting of myself?* she reasoned.

Josephine watched a sneer form at the edges of the young Peter's lips. He lifted his teacup in a salute and smirked. "Here's to you, old man! You thought you skunked me, didn't you? Well, we'll see who laughs last."

"Mr. Van der Mere," Josephine called from the doorway. At the sound of her voice, the man jumped. The woman straightened her shoulders and glided across the green and gold Oriental carpet toward the suddenly awkward young man, a determined smile pasted firmly in place. "I didn't expect to see you so soon, and especially at this late hour. I don't pretend to know European custom, but in American society it is highly irregular to come calling at such an hour." As if on cue, the hall clock gonged ten times.

Peter Jr.'s sneer broadened to a wooden grin. "In European society, the evening would be young, my dear." He took her extended hand and brushed a kiss on the back of her fingers. "When you left the city so abruptly this morning, I was concerned that I might have upset you. I fear that you and I got off on a wrong foot, so I hastened here as quickly as possible to assure you that I mean you no ill." He set the teacup down on the matching Belgium saucer.

"Won't you be seated, sir." Josephine gestured toward a Louis XIV occasional chair and seated herself on the coordinating sofa. She picked up the teapot and smiled. "May I pour you a second cup, Mr. Van der Mere?"

"No, thank you. I'm not partial to tea at this hour, ma'am." He shook his head. "Peter, please call me Peter."

"All right . . . Peter. And since we're family, please call me Josephine." She poured the hot amber liquid into the second teacup, added a smidgen of sugar and a dollop of cream. Lifting the cup to her lips, she took a sip, then paused. "Please tell me, Peter, just why are you here this evening?"

His wide, congenial grin didn't melt the hardness evident in his eyes. "I felt you and I should become acquainted, being family and all."

"We could have done that at a more reasonable hour," she chided.

The young man stared down at his hands folded in his lap. "To be honest . . . I can be honest with you, Josephine?"

"I would hope so. I cannot afford to lose any sleep listening to lies."

He shot a quick glance at her; she was smiling. He managed a stiff smile in return. "It's like this, I have recently run into several financial misfortunes. And well, I am broke!" Color climbed past his fashionably folded ascot and into his face. "I was hoping that I might have a little something coming from my father's will."

Josephine's heart was touched. She could see that it had taken a large measure of humility to admit his situation to her. Yet her husband had warned her about giving any further monies to his son. "He'll squander everything you give him on the gaming tables. He'll drain you dry. Don't give him one red cent!" Her husband's will reiterated his warnings. Legally, she couldn't give him any of her inheritance no matter how much her heart ached for the troubled young man.

She tried to explain the conditions of his father's will. "If I were to give you anything, I would lose the inheritance as well," she concluded. That's how strong your father's feelings were on the subject. I am so sorry, truly I am."

Peter drummed his fingers on the chair's upholstered arm. "I should have known! What kind of father sends his only child to live with a meddlesome aunt?"

"I understood that was your choice, Peter."

"It was better than living under his roof!"

Josephine placed the teacup on its saucer. "And he said you were well provided for."

The young man leaped to his feet and paced to the bank of windows on the far side of the room. He pulled back a sage green brocade drapery and peered out into the night. Suddenly he whirled about and snarled, "Do you know how expensive Paris is during the season?"

His sudden movement caught her off guard. Her hand flew to her neck. "I-I-I'm sure it is."

"You bet it is! But my little provincial father had no idea, nor did he care."

Josephine rose to her feet and hurried to his side. She touched his ruffled sleeve. "Oh, Peter, your father cared about you, more than you will ever know."

The man snorted. "He was too taken with his pretty little bride to care about me. That's why I was sent away—you, you were the reason."

"That's not true. I had nothing to do with it. Your father and I didn't marry until six months after you left New York."

The man narrowed his eyes into a glare and gritted his teeth. "Him and his little octaroon!"

Josephine blanched at his vicious attack. Peter moved within inches of her nose. "Tell me, did my father know he married a little colored baby? I'll bet he didn't, knowing his prejudices. Uh-uh! Not my bigoted papa." He whisked past her, strode to the fireplace, and picked up a heavy crystal paperweight. "Do you know how this got chipped? I can tell you. My father threw it at me the night I brought home a friend from school, the son of an Italian count. It seems Vincencio's skin was a little too dark for my father's liking!"

Josephine steadied herself on a nearby rosewood map stand. "What your father's prejudices might or might not have been, they are immaterial at this point. I am sorry for the wrongs you believe your father committed against you, but I can't change history, can I?"

The woman jumped when Peter slammed the paperweight down on the marble mantle.

"I don't want your pity," he snapped. "I just want what's coming to me!"

"That's the point, Peter. The will clearly states that you received your portion of your father's wealth when you left for Europe."

"Portion? I am his only son. It should have all been mine." He slammed the paperweight against the mantle a second time.

Josephine, her spine rigid with determination, replied, "And I was his only living wife."

Suddenly the drawing room doors swung open. A furious Abe filled the entrance. "What's going on in here? Are you all right, Miss Josephine? Is it time for Master Van der Mere to leave?"

"No, no . . ." The woman hastened to her servant's side. "Master Peter is telling me about his father, that's all."

Abe leveled a frightening gaze at the young man, then growled, "I hope so."

"Actually . . . ," she addressed Peter, "do you need a place to stay for the night?"

Subdued by Abe's fury and by Josephine's sudden compassion, Peter bowed his head. "Yes, ma'am, I do, if it wouldn't be too inconvenient."

"No, of course not." Josephine finally was back in her element. "Abe, please ask Dory to prepare the blue room for Master Van der Mere." She turned back to Peter. "Are you hungry? Have you had supper?"

"Madam," Abe interrupted. "I could take him down to the inn. Ben would find a—"

"Nonsense!" Josephine insisted. "Peter is a Van der Mere. He should sleep under his father's roof, at least for one night. I owe his father that much and a whole lot more."

The visitor thanked his hostess while Abe glowered. It was evident to all that Abe wasn't happy with his employer's announcement. Being the courteous gentlemen he was, Abe bowed slightly to Josephine. "As you wish, madam. Will there be anything else tonight?"

Josephine took a deep breath and smiled. "No, that will be all. Thank you." She'd never needed to stand up to her recently hired servant before. Abe might have been on an even footing with Sam, his last employer, but the man totally intimidated the diminutive Josephine.

"By the way, madam, my wife forgot to give you this." He held in his hand a letter. "It came the day you left for New York City. It's from Independence, Missouri—Miss Serenity, I presume."

"Oh!" Josephine's eyes brightened. She momentarily forgot her enigmatic guest as she gazed at the familiar handwriting. Bound together by their love for one man, the two women stayed in touch with one another by monthly letters. It was almost as if they'd become family despite the fact that Sam and Josephine had never married.

Josephine caught a movement out of the corner of her eye. She lifted her head and smiled at the visitor across the room. "A letter from my dearest friend's daughter," she explained, slipping the unopened letter into her pocket. "Please make yourself comfortable, Peter, while Dory prepares your room. Wait! You must be hungry." She picked up a nearby oil lamp, lit it from one of the candles, then gestured toward Peter. "Come to the kitchen with me and I'll slice you a piece of roast beef. A dab of Dory's horseradish sauce and a piece of her wheat bread will more than hold you 'till morning."

Uncomfortable with the unexplainable mood shift in the room, Peter stammered a thank-you. "Don't go to any trouble on my account," he added.

"Nonsense! I won't have a child of Peter's going to bed hungry in my home." She glided toward the hallway. "I hope you don't mind eating in the kitchen. I do it most of the time," she admitted.

Her dress swooshed about her ankles as she led the man into the kitchen. She lit an additional oil lamp to brighten the place, then wasted no time preparing the promised snack for her guest. She wondered what the spoiled young man was thinking as she bustled about the kitchen. She watched with pleasure as he ravenously ate the food she set before him.

Peter had barely eaten the last bite of a second slice of freshly baked bread when Dory announced that his room was ready. The thunder evident in her eyes told both of them that the servant didn't approve of the young man or the fact that he was staying the night.

"Dory, please take Mr. Van der Mere to his room. Make sure he has everything he'll need." She wished him a good night's sleep but stayed behind to straighten the kitchen. Once she'd brushed the bread crumbs into her hands and carried them to her cook's hanging bird feeder outside the back door, she returned inside and removed the letter from the envelope. Her fingers deftly opened the onion skin paper sheets of stationery. She held the letter up to the light radiating from the oil lamp.

Dearest Josephine,

Guess what? Caleb and I are going to be married. That's right—married! It will be a simple wedding compared to Eastern standards. I plan to wear a creamy ivory lace gown, one of the frocks Aunt Eunice had made for me before I left Buffalo. I never imagined when the fussy little designer was fitting the bodice to my waist that I would soon be wearing the dress at my wedding. I will cut down my rose satin dress to fit Becca, my maid-of-honor.

I wish you, Annie, Abe, and Dory could be here. I especially wish Papa . . . and Mama . . . Sometimes it's so hard without them. But God sent Uncle Eli and Aunt Fay to love me in my parents' place. And they're so kind. They couldn't treat me lovelier were I truly one of their daughters.

We appreciate being able to live at the mission. I try to help Annalee as much as I can while Aunt

Fay teaches the Indian children to read. The hotels in town are (well, should I say?) less than desirable places for families with young children to stay.

Caleb's parents are planning on leaving for California in the spring, as soon as they can "stock a wagon" as Aunt Fay says it. Caleb and I have discussed whether or not we will go with them. His dream is to set up his own blacksmith shop, and where's a better place than Independence, the wagon capitol of America? He's working for one of the blacksmiths in town right now. He's gaining a reputation in town for being honest and doing good work. Of course, for now it's just idle chatter. We want to talk it over with his folks and pray about it before we finalize such an important decision.

By next spring the telegraph lines from St. Louis will be strung. Imagine! Living in such a modern age! What will people think of next?

Please pass on the news of our upcoming wedding to Annie, Dory, and Abe. Give Annie a kiss and a hug for me. Tell her that I will write soon. There is so much to do preparing food for winter.

I was so glad to hear that Annie's hands are healing so well. I can't imagine the pain she must have gone through. The other day I burned myself removing a cover from a pot of boiling soup and I thought of Annie and what she suffered for me. Oh, how I miss her!

But then, I miss you all. Sometimes I wonder if I'll ever see any of you again, at least on this earth. New York is a long way from Missouri. However, my prayers are always with you no matter how far away you may be.

Love, Mrs. Serenity (Seri) Louise Pownell (soon-to-be) Cunard.

Josephine smiled to herself as she ran her fingertips over the signature at the end of the letter. *I would love to attend your wedding, precious one. And I miss you too.* With the troubles and confusion of the last few weeks, the tranquil vision of a little sod mission in the middle of the prairie sounded very attractive.

"What are you thinking?" Her words hung in the silence of the empty kitchen. "You're a city bred woman. You'd be a duckling out of water in such a place," she told herself. She glanced down at her carefully shaped fingernails and wrinkle-free hands. "Definitely not the life for you, missy. Not the life for you."

As she read back over the letter, she wondered again why Serenity had not received the letter she'd sent with the news of Sam's recovery. With a sigh, she folded the pages of the letter and returned it to the envelope, then stuffed it in her pocket. *I'll give the mail service another couple weeks and then I'll write her again,* she thought to herself. Carefully, she blew out the flame of the larger oil lamp and carried the small one up to her bedroom.

As she entered the room she sensed something was wrong. Her bed was turned down as always. Her chambray night dress lay folded at the foot of the massive hand-carved dark walnut four-poster bed, the bed Peter imported for her from India as a wedding gift. A lit oil lamp sat on the nightstand beside the open bed. Another lamp flickered a reflection in the dresser mirror. She gazed about the darkened room. *Someone's been in here besides Dory,* she thought as she made her way to the bay window and pulled closed the sage green satin brocade draperies.

Setting the oil lamp in her hand on an occasional table beside her Louis XIV tapestry upholstered rocker, Josephine rushed about the room, looking for definite signs of an intruder. She checked her jewelry box—everything seemed to be in order. She looked inside her bureau drawer where she kept her small collection of coins, her emergency stash, as she liked to call it. Her husband, Peter, always laughed at how protective Josephine was with her tiny treasure. Growing up poor, knowing she always had her velvet pouch of quick cash available reassured her. A quick search of the drawers in her walnut "ladies" desk revealed nothing amiss.

She returned to the windows and pulled back the edge of a drapery. She studied the dark snowy world outside her townhouse window. Except for the streetlights flickering along the avenue, all was shrouded in darkness. As she turned away, her eye caught a red glow across the street from her place, beneath a burned-out streetlamp. A red glow from a cigarette? A cigar? A pipe?

She snapped back from the window. The drapery fell into place. Someone was watching her house. A small crystal clock ticked out the minutes in the room's semidarkness. She squinted to read the time—12:04. At this hour? Who would be out there? Josephine was tempted to awaken Abe. But she knew that by the time he got dressed and out there, the stranger would be gone.

Slowly Josephine undressed. She untied the cords of her corset and dropped it and her lace-edged chemise to the floor. After sponging off in the warm water Dory had drawn for her, Josephine slipped into her night dress. As she turned down the flame on the lantern near the window, she glanced down at an empty spot beside her Bible. Her husband's gold watch was gone, both the watch and the gold fob. The glass domed display case was empty.

Peter! She shot a glance toward her bedroom door. He'd searched her room and stolen his father's watch. She shook her head in disbelief. Should she go to his room to confront him? *No*, she decided, *that would appear unseemly. What else did he steal?* she wondered as she opened her Bible. The words of John 10 comforted her. "The thief cometh not, but for to steal, and to kill, and to destroy: I am come that they might have life, and that they might have it more abundantly. I am the good shepherd: the good shepherd giveth his life for the sheep."

With a heavy heart she turned off the flames on each of the lanterns and crawled into bed. She'd barely dropped off to sleep when she heard the door of her wardrobe open and a floorboard creek. Terrified, she watched the silhouette of a man cross her room. She held her breath as he paused at the foot of her bed. *One move closer,* she vowed, *and I scream for Abe! Stepson or not!* She hesitated because she knew Abe would beat him soundly and have him dumped at the docks.

Instead of moving closer to the bed, the form turned toward the door. As he reached for the knob, Josephine mustered her courage. "Peter, I would have given your father's watch to you if you'd asked."

The man froze for an instant, then dashed from her room.

For several minutes Josephine stared into the darkness. No fire crackled in the fireplace; no embers burned red. No breeze whipped around the corners of the three-story town-house. Inside the house, all was silent as well. Only the words of the Shepherd's Psalm played through her mind. "The Lord is my Shepherd . . . ." She'd barely recited ". . . and I will dwell in the house of the Lord forever," when she fell asleep.

~7~

The
Confrontation

JOSEPHINE'S EYELIDS FLUTTERED; HER BREATH came in short gasps. Panic distorted her face as the hunting dogs barked at her heels. In the woods around her, she saw shadows of the mysterious man in black. And no matter how fast she tried to run, she wasn't moving. She looked down. Her legs were tangled in her crinolines and her feet were bare. Stubbing her toe on a log, she felt herself falling . . . falling . . . falling . . . . She tried to call for help but no sound came from her mouth. She heard someone speaking, first from far away, then closer. She thought she recognized the voice. Slowly she opened her eyes.

"Good morning, Miss Josephine," Annie's eyes sparkled with delight. "Isn't it a beautiful day? I hope I didn't waken you."

"Whatever gave you that idea?" Josephine groaned, struggling to lift her weight onto her elbows. Annie missed the woman's sarcasm. Josephine smiled to herself. Who could stay irritated with Annie and her ebullient spirit? The girl could find joy in the direst of circumstances.

Annie placed the intricately carved rosewood bed tray across Josephine's lap. "The cook sent up a tray of hot herbal tea and toast to help you start your day." The aroma from the china teapot wafted to Josephine's nostrils.

Annie continued. "She included a dish of her famous cinnamon applesauce and some strawberry preserves for the toast."

The happy young woman chattered on, leaving Josephine time to gather her wits. "Abe said that we're lucky to have gotten Viola Mae out of the house as quickly as we did. And guess what? He found your rapscallion of a stepson ransacking the contents of your desk in the library this morning."

"What?" Josephine had forgotten about the presence of Peter Van der Mere III in her home.

"Dory told me to tell you that the sooner you get that no-account scoundrel out of here the better!" Annie nodded her head for emphasis. "Those are her words, ma'am."

Josephine wiped her eyes and tried to clear her mind of the sleepers as well. "Whoa! Slow down, honey. My head is splitting. Tell me one thing at a time."

Annie swallowed hard, then started over. "Abe's staying with Mr. Van der Mere—I mean right with him—until you get down there. He won't let the man out of his sight. That's what Abe said."

Josephine blinked in bewilderment. What a way to begin another day! "Annie! Slow down."

The girl gulped. "Yes, ma'am. Dory said Abe went through the man's luggage and found several items that belong to you, including your late husband's watch. Abe called the constable already." Annie's luminous brown eyes were wide with excitement. She skipped over to the bay window; her movements were butterfly erratic. "How did he get the watch, I'd like to know. It was right here in its display case last night."

Josephine set the tray aside and leaped from the bed. "Help me dress please, Annie. I need to get downstairs before the police arrive."

Clothing flew in every direction as Annie helped Josephine into the many layers of clothing required for a decent woman to wear. As Annie fastened the last button on the back of Josephine's white embroidered blouse, the front doorbell jangled.

"Oh, no!" Josephine ran a brush through her hair and pulled it into a bun at the nape of her neck as she ran down the stairs. And Annie, her hands full of hairpins, ran to keep up with her. They made it to the first landing by the time Dory opened the front door. "Constable, I'm so glad you got here so fast. It seems we have a crook on the premises. My husband's guarding him in the drawing room. Mrs. Van der Mere will be down in a moment to join us."

"Wait!" Josephine called, hurrying down the last flight of stairs. "Thank you, Dory." She dismissed the housekeeper. The large black woman gave Josephine an I-told-you-so look and strode toward the kitchen.

Josephine whirled around to face the two policemen in the doorway. "Won't you please come in? I'm Josephine Van der Mere. And I assure you there's been some sort of mistake, or a misunderstanding between my, er, butler and my guest."

The policemen removed their hats and bowed respectfully to the lovely young woman. "I'm glad to hear that, madam. But, before we leave, we should speak with the persons involved in the altercation."

Josephine sighed but maintained her smile. "Of course. That's a very good idea. Follow me, please. Annie? Did you say they were in the breakfast nook or the drawing room?"

The girl rolled her eyes toward the spot where Dory had disappeared. "I don't know, ma'am. I think Miss Dory said the drawing room."

The lady of the house swung open the massive carved oak doors. Seated on the tapestry upholstered sofa, Peter appeared to be studying his nails, looking as unconcerned as possible with the fierce-looking Abe between him and the door.

"Here he is, miss," Abe said, rocking back on his heels in satisfaction.

Peter, tugging on his suit jacket, then adjusting his paisley cravat, arose from the sofa, a fatuous smile lingering on his face. "Thank goodness you have arrived, stepmother dear. I wouldn't have wanted to have hurt your misguided man of color." The way he emphasized the word *color* set Josephine's teeth on edge.

Josephine looked first at Peter then at Abe. The towering giant of a man outweighed Peter by a good eighty pounds. When Peter noticed the two policemen behind her, a look of uncertainty flashed across his suddenly ashen face. His eyes darted from side to side as if he were considering the odds of his escape.

Abe strode across the room to the French oak desk behind the sofa. "Miss Josephine, I found your guest going through your personal papers this morning. He'd collected a number of items and had them in this gunnysack." Abe upturned the sack onto the desktop. Out rolled a collection of expensive doodads, including two Eastern European glass paperweights made in the 1700s, a silver letter opener with the Revere insignia, a gold leaf, framed picture of her husband's first wife, a small army of iron toy soldiers dressed in Revolutionary War garb, and a brass doorstop in the shape of a cat.

The policemen's eyes narrowed as they gazed at the loot on the desk. One of the men removed his bobby stick from his belt, which spurred Peter to action.

"I didn't touch any of those things. I don't know how they got into that bag. I've never seen them before in my life!"

Josephine arched one eyebrow at Abe. "Is that all you found?"

"Oh no. Our little ne'er-do-well was busy last night. There's a whole lot more upstairs in his portmanteau, including your husband's Swiss gold watch." Abe crossed his arms and rocked back on his heels, almost daring Peter to try to make a break for it.

"I'm sure you have enough here, madam, to arrest this man for robbery," the leader of the two police officers said as he slipped a pair of metal handcuffs from his uniform pocket.

"Arrest me?" Peter snarled. "This woman's the one you should be arresting. She stole my inheritance. Everything! She's the thief, not only of my father's estate, but I've discovered that she helps runaway slaves escape to Canada! Did you know that, Officer?" Peter pointed his finger at Josephine. "She's breaking the law. Arrest her if you want to arrest anyone."

Peter folded his arms across his chest in satisfaction. "What I was doing was looking for evidence of her wrongdoing. Arrest her! She and her fiancé, Samuel Pownell, ran an illegal operation right here under your noses."

"Assemblyman Pownell?" The second policeman's eyes narrowed at the mention of Sam's name. He studied the elegant woman standing beside him, then the miscreant making the accusations.

"Yep! That's the one." Peter flashed an arrogant grin at Josephine.

The policeman's eyes narrowed further, his forehead riddled with lines. "The same one they voted out of the state assembly last fall?"

"Yep! That's the one!" Peter looked delighted with himself. A sarcastic smirk crossed his face. It was evident to Josephine that he intended to bury her and in the process, gain access to his father's wealth.

Josephine cleared her throat. Things weren't going well. She cast an apprehensive glance at Abe. If these two policemen did a thorough search of the premises, they would find more than enough suspicious evidence in the attic to alert the authorities to their suspicions. Cots, blankets, discarded clothing, and water barrels in the attic and the basement would lend credence to Peter's charges.

"Assemblyman Pownell, eh?" The first policeman smiled down at the diminutive blonde. "I heard he drowned in a storm off South Carolina. A terrible loss. He was a good man."

She blinked in surprise.

"He and his wife used to bring gallons of hot apple cider and dozens of Christmas cookies to the station every Christmas Eve. We'll sure miss it this year."

The second policeman nodded. "And they were the best gingersnaps you ever put in your mouth." His eyes grew hard as he focused on Peter's face. "What do you want us to do with this man, Mrs. Van der Mere?"

"Nothing at all," she replied.

"Nothing?" Abe and the two policemen exclaimed in unison. Even Peter looked surprised.

"Nothing. First of all, last night I gave Peter his father's watch. Didn't I, Peter?" Josephine arched her eyebrow and cocked her head to one side, daring Peter to refute her claim. The accused man had the decency to blush. "And as for this little collection here in the gunnysack, I want him to have these things. They belonged to his father. And, I suspect, the toy soldiers were probably his as a child." She paused a moment, frowned, then added, "But wait, I have something else in the wall safe—your mother's wedding ring and your great-grandmother's silver diamond necklace. They should be yours as well, to give to your future wife, whoever she may be."

Josephine started toward the painting behind which was the hidden safe when Peter mumbled, "I already have them and these too." He reached into his coat pocket and withdrew a set of pearl earrings with a matching necklace.

Josephine searched his face for a trace of remorse but found none. "Keep the pearls, Peter, and whenever you look at them, think of me." Her skirts rustled as she turned toward the policemen. "I think we're done here. Would you please escort my house guest to the depot? I believe Mr. Van der Mere has a morning train for New York City to catch. I would hate to have him miss it, officers."

"But Missy . . ." Abe interrupted. She smiled at the frustrated servant, patting his hand gently.

"It's all right, my friend. It is better this way." She turned to Peter. "Peter, I never want to see you back here again asking for money. Do you understand?"

The man's obsequious smile faded into a sneer. "You may get the best of me today," he snarled, "but I'm not finished with you yet, you little octoroon!"

Outraged, Abe lunged for Peter, but the police interceded. "We've got him, ma'am. And we will personally make sure he boards the train for New York City this morning," the first policeman said, while the second policeman clapped a pair of handcuffs on Peter's wrists. One on each side, the officers grabbed Peter's arms and hustled him toward the front door.

"Don't forget his portmanteau," Abe called, running after the policemen with Peter's suitcase.

"And the gunnysack," Josephine added, handing Abe the bag with the items purloined from her home.

"What a way to start a new day, eh, Missy?" Dory chuckled as the policemen led Peter Van der Mere off to the paddy wagon.

"Huh? Oh, you startled me, Dory." Josephine slipped her hand into the crook of her housekeeper's arm. "It's kind of sad, isn't it? What happens from the time a little boy plays with tin soldiers and he grows to be a man? What makes the difference in the outcome?"

Dory gave a gentle snort. "Sages of the centuries have tried to determine the answer to that question."

Josephine blinked back a rush of tears. "I wish things could have been different between us. It would have been nice having family around."

"Hmmph! Better such family be strangers if you ask me!" Dory sputtered, her hands resting resolutely on her comfortably protruding stomach. "That boy be trouble no matter how you count it."

Josephine sighed and nodded in agreement. She knew the woman was right. Peter Van der Mere III would bring nothing but trouble in her life. "And I'm afraid we haven't seen the last of him. It's not good that he knows about the Underground Railroad station here. Maybe I've worn out my usefulness to the cause."

"Don't be saying things like that, Missy. Think of all the good you've done. Think about little Viola Mae who is probably safe in Canada by now thanks to you."

Josephine smiled sadly. "Sometimes my husband's legacy is more of a curse than a blessing. He made the bulk of it, you know, as owner of the ships that transported slaves to the Carolinas."

"And you are using that money to help slaves escape to freedom," Dory nodded wisely. "Somehow, there's justice in that, don't you think?"

Josephine smiled in spite of her heavy heart at the delicious irony in the fact that Peter Van der Mere II's legacy was used to aid the children and grandchildren of those he used to increase his riches. "God is a God of surprises, isn't He?" Josephine turned to reenter the house.

Dory patted the woman's shoulder. "Yes, ma'am, He surely is."

"When Abe comes inside," Josephine began, "I need to talk with him. I'll be in the library."

"Yes, ma'am," Dory grinned. "I'll send him right in."

"Thank you." Josephine glided into the library and closed the double doors behind her. Crossing the Oriental carpet to the window, she drew back the draperies. The early morning sunlight flooded through the tall and narrow, diamond-leaded windows. She watched the paddy wagon pull away from the front of her home and Abe walk up the steps to the house. She also noticed a man standing in the shadows of the house on the corner across the street from hers, a man dressed in a long black riding coat, his hat pulled down over his forehead, shading his eyes.

"Abe!" she called, running for the library doors.

"What?" Abe burst into the room. His eyes were wide with fear. "What is it, Missy?"

"That man. That man I told you about from the train and from the inn the other night? He's across the street."

Without a pause, Abe bounded from the room. Josephine ran to the window and watched her friend dash across the snowy street. In a flash, the man in black disappeared down the alleyway. Abe raced to catch up with him.

"Oh, dear God, protect Abe from this frightening man. Keep him safe." Josephine remained by the window until she saw Abe limping out of the alleyway several minutes later.

She gave a squeal of distress. "Dory! Abe's been hurt!" Josephine ran out the front door and down the steps to the slate sidewalk. The slush in the streets penetrated her soft doeskin house slippers, but she didn't stop until she reached her friend's side. "Abe! You've been hurt. What happened? Are you all right?"

"My bum leg!" Disgusted, he reached down and rubbed the leg he'd broken last summer at Lake Cayuga. "It gave out on me before I could get close enough for a decent look at him. But I'll get him next time, Missy, I promise."

Josephine put an arm around Abe and coaxed him to lean on her. The giant of a man laughed. "On you, Missy? I'd squash you like a June bug."

"I'm stronger than I look," she argued. Together they hobbled across the road to the front steps where Dory came bursting out of the townhouse.

"What fool thing were you doing, Old Man?"

Abe tried to explain, but Dory was not in an "explainin' mood" as she called it. "I don't want to hear about it. Send one of the young bucks from the stables to do your police work next time."

"There wasn't time," Abe argued. The whine in Abe's voice brought a chuckle from Josephine. It seemed so incongruous with his massive size. But around Dory, everyone, including Abe, became one of her chickens to protect.

"I was afraid the man would get away," he protested.

"Like he did, right?" his wife added. "Get on in here and let me rub some lotion on that leg. You should know better. You ain't no spring buck any longer."

"It was my fault, Dory. I wasn't thinking," Josephine said.

"Hmmph!" Dory interrupted. "It weren't your fault. If I've told Abe once, I've told him a thousand times not to try to do everything himself. He's got men here to help. It's not like he has to do everything around here."

Abe allowed his wife to help him into the house. "I did send James after the mail this morning," he replied.

"Only so you could keep tabs on Mr. Van der Mere," Dory reminded.

"I don't like this guy snooping around," Abe warned, despite his wife's ministrations. "And your stepson's threats? There was hate in his voice. He's serious. And we need to take him seriously."

"I know, Abe," Josephine replied, "but, don't worry about that right now."

"It's my job to worry. That's what Mr. Sam asked me to do, remember?"

Josephine smiled sadly at the mention of Sam Pownell. When would she ever see him again? She'd been praying hard for his return to his normal robust health.

"I'm thinking," Abe began, "that we should close down the station for a few months until we're sure your stepson has moved on."

Josephine groaned. While she'd been thinking the same thought earlier, she hated hearing it voiced. "I hate to allow him to interfere."

"You're not the only one at risk. If Van der Mere brings

in the law, good people all the way from Georgia to the Canadian border will be compromised."

"Abe, you and Miss Josephine can talk about this later. For right now, let me see to your leg," Dory sputtered.

Josephine watched the two disappear down the hallway. She thanked the Lord for bringing such a faithful and caring couple into her life.

~8~

The Letter

A<small>FTER</small> J<small>OSEPHINE</small> <small>SAT DOWN TO HER DESK,</small> she rearranged the ink well and pens, part of her routine each month at bill-paying time. She'd moved the desk to the bank of diamond lead-paned windows after her husband died. She enjoyed watching the traffic roll by outside the window. Peter preferred having it closer to the fireplace for warmth. Josephine loved watching the world go by on Capitol Boulevard. Gilded carriages of the wealthy, farm wagons loaded with produce, fashionable two-passenger cabriolets, and men on horseback—a never-ending parade of life was hers for the enjoyment during the warm months of the year. When snow filled the roadway, she enjoyed watching cozy, two-person sleighs and the larger cutters glide down the street toward the marketplace in the center of the city.

On this November day, with the unseasonable snow turning to slush, there would be little traffic to distract her from balancing her housekeeping books, a task that was one of her least favorite she'd inherited from her wealthy husband. If it hadn't been for Charity Pownell, the job would have remained incomprehensible to the young woman who had always carried the sum of her treasure in a hidden pocket in the folds of her linsey-woolsey skirts.

Josephine smiled to herself. "Who would think how much one Christian woman could affect so many people's lives?" She sighed heavily at the memory of the woman who'd been like a sister to her. "Oh, how I miss you, Charity," she breathed into the stillness of the room.

It was mid-morning before Josephine's stomach growled with hunger. She glanced at the mantle clock. "Ten-thirty? Is that all?" Remembering the haste in which she left her room earlier without eating, she strode to the library doors and pulled the tapestry servant cord suspended on the wall beside the left door. She was back at her desk before Cora, one of the kitchen maids, answered her call.

"Yes, ma'am?" The brawny Dutch lass bobbed a curtsy.

Josephine glanced up from her ledger. "Cora, please bring a pot of hot cocoa and a plate of shortbread cookies to my room? I'm a wee bit sleepy this morning. I think I'll take a short nap."

"Yes, ma'am. Right away. Would you like a poached egg or a sweet roll? The cook just finished making an apple crisp for dinner."

"No, thank you. I'll save that for later. But a fresh apple would be nice."

"Yes, ma'am." The girl whirled about and disappeared down the hallway to the kitchen.

Josephine padded across the carpet, across the shiny beige marble floor in the foyer, and up the carved oak staircase to her room. As she passed the room where Peter had stayed, sadness invaded her heart almost as if she'd had a death in the family. *A soft answer didn't turn away his wrath, that's for sure,* she thought as she hurried on to her bedroom on the opposite end of the open staircase.

Josephine had barely made herself comfortable in her rocker by the window and opened her Bible to the book of John when Cora arrived with the tray of food.

"James gave me the packet of mail for you, madam." Cora set the tray on the stand beside Josephine's rocker, then removed a bulging pouch of letters from her apron pocket.

Josephine chose one of the English shortbread cookies on the dainty blue-and-white china cake plate and took a bite. She closed her eyes in ecstasy.

"Delicious as usual." When Cora tried to hand her the letters, she waved them away. "Place them on the bed, please. I'll read the letters later. And tell the cook that these cookies are her best ever."

"Yes, madam." The maid giggled and curtsied shyly. "You say that every time, madam."

Josephine grinned. "Yes, I guess I do. But I really do mean it," she hastened to add. "These lovely little things literally melt in my mouth."

Between nibbles on her shortbread cookies, Josephine read the tenth chapter of John, where she'd quit reading the night before. "I am the good shepherd; the good shepherd giveth his life for the sheep. . . ." She read for several minutes, then paused to think about the message in the words she'd read. "No man taketh [my life] from me, but I lay it down of myself."

Kneeling beside the rocker, Josephine prayed, "Lord, in Your time, You laid down Your life for me. Thank You for that sacrifice. I give my life to You today. Help me to know Your will, what direction You want me to go."

She paused for a moment to wipe the gathering tears from her eyes. "Sometimes I feel so alone, Father, and lost. With Peter scrutinizing my every move and this mystery man hovering nearby, I feel like a butterfly under a microscope. Am I putting others at risk? I don't know what to do."

She remembered how Charity scolded her whenever she said anything about being alone. "Josephine, don't say that! You are a child of God. You are never alone."

Josephine continued her prayer. "I know I'm not alone, but I am the one who has to decide what I should do next, Lord. But until You direct, I will be still and know that You are who You claim to be."

After a few moments she rose to her feet. A wave of peace washed over her troubled spirit. She felt refreshed, invigorated. She decided a nap wasn't what she needed after all. Her gaze fell on the packet of mail laying on the foot of her bed. She walked across the room, picked up the packet, and untied the string holding the letters together. One by one, she shuffled through the stack. A bill from her milliner for a new spring bonnet, a bill from the blacksmith for repairing a broken carriage spring, another from Farmer Cooper for oats and hay for her team of horses.

Her eyes brightened when she spotted a familiar handwriting on a rather large envelope toward the bottom of the stack—S.P. and postmarked New Orleans, Louisiana. This was only the second letter she'd received from Sam Pownell personally since he left her in Auburn.

Tossing the rest of the letters onto her bed, her hands trembled with excitement as she broke the seal on the treasured envelope and withdrew the letter. Butterflies fluttered and did somersaults in her stomach at the sight of the familiar handwriting. A tear trickled, unbidden, down her cheek as she read the return address. S.P., c/o Miss Clare Thornton, Cypress Lane, New Orleans, Louisiana.

"Dearest Josephine," the letter began. Her heart pounded in her ears. Even now, she still couldn't believe Sam was really alive! She remembered the day the announcement arrived. She'd laughed; she'd cried; she'd fainted on the floor. Keeping the news a secret from everyone but Abe had been the most difficult task he'd ever required of her. When she told Abe about the letter, he wouldn't believe it either until he read the letter for himself.

Josephine had reread the letter so many times in the last two months her tears had smudged the ink. "Oh Lord . . ." She clutched the letter to her breast. "I praise You! I praise You! I praise You! You are so good to Your children."

She ran to the bedroom door and closed it, pirouetting in the middle of the floor several times. She felt like a school girl receiving her first love note. She didn't care, knowing he was safe was all that mattered. She sniffed the paper, hoping to inhale the lingering aroma of her loved one. Her imagination did the rest.

She curled up in the middle of the bed with her legs crossed and began to read the letter.

It has been too long since I've been able to write to you. My right arm has been giving me trouble this fall. The weather in New Orleans has been cool and damp. Give me a good snowstorm any day.

There's so much to tell you, most of which cannot be written for fear of it being intercepted by the wrong people. I am up and about now.

That's progress. As to my leg—I will always walk
with a cane, I fear.

When my good Samaritan brought me to
Clare Thornton's place after I'd been beaten and
left for dead in the woods, I wasn't expected to
live. Clare, my nurse and my savior, tells me that I
was in and out of consciousness for many days.
But I guess I have more to do before the grim
reaper makes his call because this old body seems
to be on the mend.

Josephine smiled to herself, picturing the tall, strong
man Sam had always been. She continued reading.

I told you about Clare in the last letter. She is
a former schoolteacher and feels as strongly about
our cause as do we. She and a few of her faithful
friends have risked a lot to care for me.

My presence here adds additional risk to her
cause as well. I know the neighbors have questioned her about the "cousin" living with her.
One Sunday I ventured to church with her—big
mistake! Too many questions asked.

Josephine started at the idea of Sam attending church
for any reason. "Clare, you must be one persuasive lady to
get Sam inside a church." She returned her attention to the
letter.

As to my living expenses, I've been able to put
my hands on some funds, thanks to concerned
friends in Auburn. They tell me that my brother
didn't waste any time selling off my assets once he
heard I was dead. Ah, family! Also, I heard about

the vote of censure in the state assembly. It hurt
more than I imagined it could. We've paid a
mighty price for our compassion, haven't we? And
sometimes I wonder if I've chosen the right way
to go about it.

Josephine stared at the words in disbelief. She felt a
sharp pain in her chest. She and Sam had risked everything
to help those poor runaways and now he was doubting that
choice? She'd never doubted, not for one minute, that what
she was doing was right, even risking the friendship of Jon
and Geneva Morland. That she was "one of them" might
have something to do with it. *Maybe,* she thought, *maybe
Sam couldn't completely understand, he being white. . . .*
Everything had been so clear before Sam left. Their mission; their love; their future together. With a heavy heart,
she continued reading.

Thanks to Clare, much has changed in my life,
which brings me to the purpose of this letter.
Things were moving fast before I left New York,
too fast. Having to remain confined to a bed for a
spell has given me time to slow down and think
about my life and what I want to do with what's
left of it.

A cold chill passed through Josephine. She didn't like
the tone. Had his feelings for her changed? Had he fallen in
love with his nurse, Clare Thornton? Had she lost him forever? Josephine squeezed shut her eyes, trying to dislodge
the image of a pretty young schoolteacher ministering to the
needs of her fiancé. "Dear Lord, forgive me for my hateful
thoughts. After all, she did save his life, for which I am very
grateful."

She returned to the letter.

> I have a large sum of money entrusted to my solicitor, Mr. Cox, in Albany. Could you arrange to have Abe deliver it to me? I've written out the necessary information which will allow Cox to release it to you. He'll set you up with gold pieces and with bank notes.
>
> You'll have to be the one to see Mr. Cox since no bank official would entrust such money to the care of a Negro. If the two of you can contrive a way for Abe to travel with the money without drawing attention to its existence, that would help. I know this is a risk, but I'm sure Abe can handle it.

Josephine's heart quickened. *Send Abe? Why should Abe go to Sam? Abe has a wife and a son to care for, along with the place here. I'm the one who should go. I'm the one who's free to go wherever I want and do whatever I care to do.* She wriggled her nose in indignation.

> Travel at this time of year can be treacherous either by land or sea, but receiving this money is of the utmost importance. I don't know of anyone other than Abe whom I would trust to carry out this task.

"What about me, you stinker?" Her voice echoed back into her own ears. He ended the letter by thanking Josephine for her faithful friendship. He warned her to be careful. "There's a chance you're being watched. I know I sound strange worrying about such things, but there are very few people you can trust in this world."

She stared at the piece of linen paper in her hand. No mention of loving her—no mention of asking her to come to him—no mention of the plans they'd made together less than six months ago. Tears slid down her cheeks, splotching the ink on the letter. She paced across the room, her steps those of an old woman instead of the twenty-nine-year-old that she was.

As she passed the mirror in the corner by the bedroom door, she caught a glimpse of her drawn, sallow face. In her mind she saw a wrinkled old woman, twenty years hence, still waiting for her fiancé to return. The woman burst into a flood of tears.

"Clare Thornton, whoever you are, I hate you! But I also love you for saving Sam's life. Oh, I don't know what to think!" She threw herself on the bed and pounded her fist into a pillow. "It's not fair, Lord. I love Sam. I really do. And I miss him so much." She wrapped her arms about her stomach and rocked from side to side. "He was mine for such a short time, Lord. How can I survive losing him again?"

A voice in her mind reminded her that Sam was never hers. *No one person can own another. Only God has the right to own Sam, not you. Pray for him, that God will own him as God owns you.*

Josephine obeyed the voice. She paused in her grief to lift up before God, Sam's soul. As God's peace seeped into her mind, she relaxed. She didn't stir until she heard Annie call her name. "Miss Josephine, will you be wanting lunch in your room?"

Josephine sat up and rubbed her red and swollen eyes. Annie gasped. "Oh, Missy, you've been crying. Are you in pain? Is there anything I can do?"

"No, no . . . there's nothing anyone can—" She stopped and scowled. A plan was forming in her mind, an extension of her dreams. "Oh, yes there is! Annie, please have Abe send one of the hands for my gray humpbacked trunk. And I'll need my hand luggage from the attic."

The girl's eyes widened with wonder. "Are you going somewhere, Miss Josephine?"

"I'm going to New Orleans, Annie. Would you like to go with me?" Not waiting for an answer, Josephine bounced off the bed, ran to her wardrobe, and threw open the doors. "Now, let's see, what will I need to take with me. Oh yes, and please have Dory assemble the household staff. I need to speak with them."

"Y-y-yes, Miss Josephine. And yes, I'd love to go with you." Annie bobbed a curtsy and hurried to carry out her assignment.

Annie had barely exited the room when Josephine sashayed across the room to the abandoned letter. "If you think I'll send Abe instead of coming to you myself, Samuel Pownell, you don't know me very well! And if you think I will give you up without a fight, you are wrong again, Mr. Samuel Pownell. I love you. If you don't love me anymore, that's all right, but you're going to have to tell me to my face."

"Excuse me, Miss Josephine?" Annie's timid voice called from the doorway. "Did you call me?"

"Oh, no! Sorry. I'm just thinking out loud." Josephine reddened, but her determination didn't falter.

Annie broke into a wide grin. "I love to travel, especially with you."

"Well, get ready for a boat trip."

"A boat?"

"A ship, really. We're taking a clipper ship to Louisiana. And the sooner the better!"

Josephine marveled that Annie never paused to ask why they were going to New Orleans. She was ready to go without explanation. "A great example of trust, Lord, isn't she? Go without asking why? I hope I'm doing the right thing. Please make it the right thing."

***

Josephine's announcement to the staff regarding Samuel Pownell's sudden resurrection brought a "Glory be!" from Dory and tears of joy from Annie.

"You knew and you didn't tell me?" Dory punched her husband's arm. "Since when are you keeping secrets from your wife?"

"It wasn't my secret to tell, Precious," he reminded, giving her a squeeze.

"Well," she huffed, pretending to be piqued at him, "I could never keep a secret like that from you."

A sad little smile flitted across Josephine's face as she watched the interaction between the spatting middle-aged couple. She felt a niggling guilt in her heart for not carrying out Sam's instructions as he requested, but another part of her mind convinced her she was doing the right thing by going to Sam.

The announcement set off a flurry of questions among the staff, not the least of which was from Abe. Josephine traveling to Louisiana without him? No woman could travel that distance alone! He voiced his objections strongly, but Josephine stood firm.

"You can't go, Abe, what with your leg like it is," Josephine argued, knowing Dory would agree. "Sea travel at this time of year? You'd be crippled with pain before you reached Charleston, let alone New Orleans."

"I could manage!" he snarled.

"She's right, honey." Dory chose a more sympathetic voice to persuade her husband. "But," Dory shook her head, "I don't like you going off by yourselves either. It's not good. Who knows what might happen to two girls traveling alone? Can't you wait a few months until the weather is more pleasant?"

"No, Sam needs me. And he has some very important business he asked me to attend to, business that can't wait for another few months." Josephine gazed at the worried faces about her. There was little doubt that they loved her and were worried for her safety, but she remained adamant. "And I've been thinking, Abe. With this mysterious man hanging around and Peter's threats this morning, you may be right about closing down the station for a time. We don't want to endanger other people's lives."

Abe glowered. His eyes narrowed to two angry slits. He hated having her turn around his own arguments and use them on him. After a short pause, he nodded his head sagely. "I will concede to the plan if James or one of the livery hands could go with you as protection."

Josephine pursed her lips. A tiny smile formed at the edges. "That might be a good idea. He would bunk in the servants' quarters aboard ship. Of course, Annie will stay with me in my cabin."

Abe heaved a giant sigh, rose to his feet, and hobbled toward the door. "I'll see which of the men would be willing to make the trip. When will you want to leave, Missy?"

"I want to go to him as quickly as possible."

"That's what I'd want to do if I were Missy and it were

my man needing me!" Dory nodded her head for emphasis. "And you know I would too."

"Yeah, well . . ." Abe acted embarrassed by her honesty.

Josephine removed a tiny silver pocketwatch from her skirt pocket and gazed at the face. "I can't carry out Sam's request today, and I will want to take some provisions with us, especially medicines we might need. Wednesday? Could we leave for New York on Wednesday morning and sail on Thursday perhaps?"

"I'll take care of the arrangements, Missy," Abe volunteered. "I'll telegraph for reservations. Will you be staying over with the Morlands?"

Josephine shook her head sadly. "I don't think that would be a good idea right now. I'll arrange for letters of introduction from my lawyer, Mr. Jeffreys. That should get me into any reputable hotel."

Women traveling and staying in a public hotel alone was not only unheard of, but illegal. Regardless of her age she needed either a letter of permission from her husband or her father. The presence of James, the livery hand, was not enough since he was a mere servant, not her equal.

After thanking Abe for his help, Josephine assigned each of the staff members tasks that needed to be done before her departure. She began with her laundress. "Bertha, I need the lavender cotton damask dress I took to New York and my blue silk crepe as well. As to the usual crinolines and undergarments, it will be cold aboard ship. That reminds me, Annie, don't forget we need to pack my blue woolen cape as well."

"I'll pack a couple baskets of food." The cook's rosy cheeks glowed. "You'll need peppermint tea to ward off the sniffles." The woman was her happiest when needed.

"They do feed us aboard ship," Josephine reminded.

"You call that food?" The woman looked indignant. "Fodder!"

Josephine laughed out loud. "I'm sure we'll appreciate your efforts. Be sure to include a couple jars of applesauce and some of your yummy soda crackers."

Delighted with her assignment, the cook bustled from the room, the three kitchen maids following after her like baby ducklings following their mother.

When Josephine finished, Dory took over, mumbling between her instructions how she couldn't believe that Mister Sam was truly alive.

Josephine and Annie spent the rest of the day packing and repacking their trunks. One crinoline or two? How many bonnets would they need to take? How many pairs of woolen stockings to wear on those cold nights aboard ship? So many unknowns. It wasn't until Josephine sent Annie to bed and she flopped on her bed, exhausted, that she began to doubt the wisdom of her hasty decision. What if Sam rejected her upon seeing her? No, she reasoned, he'd be too much of a gentleman to do a thing like that. What if he'd already made Clare Thornton his bride? No, again, Sam was a gentleman, not a cad, she realized. Other questions arose in her mind. What if she put Annie's life at risk, just to accomplish her own selfish ends? That thought sobered her. She didn't worry about the danger such a journey might be to her, but to Annie? Annie had been through so much in her short life.

Tiptoeing quietly up the stairs to the servants' quarters, Josephine knocked gently on the girl's bedroom door. "Annie? Are you still awake?"

"Yes, ma'am." The door opened wide. Annie greeted her with a big smile, even after the exhausting day they'd been through. "Is something wrong? Can I do something for you?" the little maid asked.

"No, I couldn't sleep thinking about you. You do understand the risk we'll be taking making this journey at this time of year, don't you? It could be dangerous."

Annie's eyes sparkled. "I won't tell you that the idea of traveling by ship doesn't frighten me; it does. But that won't stop me from going with you."

"Are you sure?" Josephine urged.

"Oh, yes, Miss. You're the bravest woman I know, after Charity, that is, and if you're going to New Orleans, Louisiana, then I want to go too. It's not like we're going alone. Didn't you tell me that God promised He'd never leave us or forsake us?"

— 9 —

On Board

IN THE STEAM AND CONFUSION OF THE TRAIN
station they said their good-byes. Abe, Dory,
Annie, James, and Josephine. Abe and Dory
hugged Annie as if they'd never see her again.
A chill traversed Josephine's spine as she realized that their fears
might be proven true. There were many miles of rail and water
between Albany and New Orleans. Anything could happen.

How beautiful Annie looked in her cocoa brown woolen
cape and matching bonnet, the color of her luminous
almond-shaped eyes. The girl was excited and eager to
begin her adventure. She clutched her portmanteau in one
hand and her railway ticket in the other. Dory sobbed
openly while Abe cleared his throat and snorted into his red
print handkerchief.

And James, poor James . . . Josephine smiled in spite of
the melancholy air surrounding their departure. The livery
boy of twenty eyed the massive growling monster of a train
as if it were a creature of doom. Josephine made a mental
note to replace his ill-fitting coat and patched trousers once
they reached New York City.

As for Josephine herself, pain rose in her chest knowing
she'd caused the grief her dear friends were feeling. She

smoothed an imaginary wrinkle in the skirt of her gray woolen traveling suit, running her fingers along the navy blue silk braid down the front of the waist-cinching jacket. The brisk wind coming off the bay ruffled her curls but couldn't ruffle her heavy skirts due to the cotton pouches sewn into the linings of her skirt and crinolines. Similar pouches were sewn into the linings of other garments stowed in her two travel trunks. She would safely deliver Sam's treasure to him one way or another.

When Abe protested again that he should be making the journey, not her, Josephine's hands fluttered to a stray curl teasing the end of her nose in the breeze.

"It will be fine, Abe." Speaking above the station noises, she amended her vow to say, "We will be fine. I'll send a telegram as soon as we dock in New Orleans, I promise."

Whistles blew. The trainmen called to one another along the track; the conductor started shutting the doors to the carriages. Quick hugs and kisses and the threesome climbed on board. The great wheels squealed and groaned as they started to turn; steam hissed, and the train inched out of the station.

Josephine and Annie waved until they could no longer see the middle-aged couple waving from the platform. Josephine glanced about the carriage. Except for a couple with three young daughters and two businessmen reading the morning paper, the carriage was empty.

"James? Where's James? I have his ticket in my purse. James? James?" she called.

"Back here, Miss Josephine." The gangly young man stood up, his jaw set with determination as he clutched his seat with one hand and the seat in front of him with the other.

"Are you all right, James?" Josephine asked, wondering if bringing the young man along would cause her more problems than he was worth.

"I'll be fine. I just can't stand on my feet too well with this contraption moving." He swayed from side to side. "Iron horse? Give me a real live horse any day over this beast."

Josephine laughed. "Don't worry, you'll get used to it after a while, I promise." She laughed again. "Wait until you get on board the schooner."

He rolled his gray-blue eyes toward the ceiling in resignation as the train rounded a curve and plunked him down in his seat.

By the time the train pulled into the depot in New York City, all three travelers were tired and uncomfortable. Except for stops to take on fuel and to let passengers on and off in little hamlets along the Hudson River valley, they'd been riding for seven hours. Josephine blessed Abe's thoughtfulness and care when a rented carriage and driver were there to meet them at the station and take them to a hotel for the night. He'd taken care of everything for her, as he promised. She had to admit to herself that she would have felt a whole lot better about the trip if he could have come along.

As the carriage rolled past the Morlands' townhouse, warm inviting lights shown from the downstairs windows. For a moment Josephine considered stopping to tell them about Sam, but the uncertainty of her welcome held her back. She leaned back against the smooth leather seating and vowed she'd send them a telegram from Baltimore or Norfolk.

By the look on James's face, Josephine suspected he was homesick already. Her stomach growled. *And probably famished too,* she thought. She withdrew her silver pocket watch from her vest pocket and checked the time—7:51. Dinnertime. They'd devoured the cook's basket of goodies hours ago.

They checked into the hotel. Her lawyer's letter of introduction was sufficient for the hotel proprietor. James's and Annie's eyes widened in surprise when Josephine ordered dinner from the bell porter and had it delivered to their suite. Josephine knew that if she'd dined in the hotel's fine restaurant, James, and especially Annie, would not be welcome.

As the three of them sat at the carefully appointed table wheeled in by an immaculately dressed waiter, Josephine said, "James, tomorrow before we board the packet for New Orleans, we need to get you some new clothing."

The boy choked on a piece of chicken breast. He coughed and shook his head emphatically. "Oh, no, ma'am, I'd really rather not."

Even Annie stopped eating and stared in surprise. "But why?" Josephine asked.

"Master Abe tried to get me fancied up in Albany and I told him the same thing. I feel better wearing my own duds."

"Are you sure? If it's the cost—"

"No, ma'am, it's not the cost. I'd feel awkward wearing someone else's clothes."

Josephine patted her lips with the linen napkin. "All right, as you wish."

Annie and Josephine slept in the large bedroom while James was given a small servant's quarters off the suite's parlor. In the morning she was surprised to find him sleeping on the floor. When she asked him about it, he reddened. "I know I'm a stubborn cuss, but I ain't never slept in a bed."

"You have a cot in the servants' quarters back in Albany," Josephine protested.

"No, I had Abe take it out of the tack room so's I had room to stretch out on the floor. I hope it don't upset you," he defended. "I'll sleep in a bed if you like."

Josephine laughed. "James, you may sleep on the floor, in a bed, wherever you like."

"Thank you, ma'am." He nodded shyly.

They left the hotel in a flurry. They would be traveling on a clipper ship built for the California run. Fast and sleek, they would be in New Orleans in seven days, barring storms or other disasters.

Their carriage driver arrived at the vessel as the ship's steward rang the first bell. Well-dressed men and women climbed the gangplank while waving to family and friends standing on the wharf.

The sound of sawing and hammering echoed across the docks as the three rushed across the wharf. The smell of wood shavings and pitch accosted Josephine's nostrils. New York was becoming the fastest growing ship building port on the East Coast. Crowds stood on the docks watching the drama unfold. Rowboats and sailboats dotted the harbor. Josephine craned her neck to see the top of the ship's mid-mast, which rose more than a hundred feet into the air.

A tall, pasty-looking steward wearing a navy blue uniform stood at the top of the gangway taking the passengers' tickets. He waved Josephine and Annie one direction and James the other. She'd tried to arrange for him a small room in the servants' quarters, but all they had available was a place in steerage.

"It's all right, Mrs. Van der Mere," James said, "I'll be more comfortable there anyway." As he walked in the direction indicated, Josephine noticed the slight wobble to his gait. She smiled sadly. She'd hoped James would enjoy his first trip outside of Albany, but so far, he'd been nothing but uncomfortable.

Due to California's gold rush, the *Sea Wren*, a tea clipper, weighing 1,215 tons, had been diverted from the China route. These lightweight clippers could make the run from New York to China in record time. When merchandise was needed to support the search for gold in California, American ship owners were in the best position to take advantage of the event. And the race was on.

A sister ship, the *Sea Witch*, had broken the earlier record of two hundred days from New York to San Francisco. But the *Sea Wren* was in no such rush. She carried tons of merchandise for the California miners from the factories in Massachusetts and Connecticut. The ship was built to withstand the violent weather off Cape Horn.

Twenty-five cabin passengers and forty steerage boarded the ship that afternoon, most of whom were heading for California's gold fields. Later that evening before sailing on the tide, Josephine dined alone in the small cabin class dining saloon since neither Annie nor James felt much like eating any food.

The clipper ship's advertising claimed the vessel served delicious and nutritious food. After a few bites of soggy crackers and a couple of spoonfuls of diluted clam chowder, Josephine decided she'd retire to her cabin for a good night's sleep.

As the clipper ship set sail at midnight, Annie and Josephine were awakened by the shouts of sailors and the clank of the anchor chain.

"Are you all right?" she whispered to Annie.

A weak "uh-huh" came from the other berth.

"Are you sure?" Josephine asked again.

"I think so."

"How can you be sick? We've barely left the dock?"

"I don't know, but I just am."

As for Josephine, Peter Van der Mere II had taught his young wife to love sailing on the tall and graceful ships. Being on board a ship once more was like coming home to the young woman. She loved the sea air. She loved the excitement of watching the sails billow in the wind. She loved the way the ship skimmed across the waves as if it had wings. Josephine loved everything about sea travel. She and her former husband had taken several day cruises together. They'd talked about making the journey to England, but Peter had died before they could do so.

Annie, however, had proven to be another story. Before the ship had left the harbor, she was stretched out on her bunk, looking decidedly green. Josephine couldn't help but wonder if she'd made a horrid mistake bringing Annie and James with her.

"Was I being selfish, Lord?" She waited, almost expecting a verbal answer from the sky, but none came. "I was, wasn't I?"

Guilt tortured the fringes of her mind. She admitted to herself that she'd hardly given God a voice in her decision. She'd made her choice to go to Sam and expected God to ordain it.

Josephine remained awake until she heard Annie's gentle snoring. Worried about James, Josephine arose from her berth, dressed in her warmest clothes, and slipped out of her cabin. As she stepped out onto the deck, a crisp breeze stung her cheeks. She tightened the laces on her bonnet and pulled the hood of her woolen cape closer to her face. How she'd find James in the darkness, she didn't know.

Heavy ponderous clouds overcast the sky. A heavy fog bank

obliterated light from any man- or God-made lights. A brisk wind whipped about her shoulders. They were in for a storm before morning, she was certain. The clipper sailed across the running sea as if racing the gale toward calmer waters.

Ocean spray bit at her face as she clung to the railing and stared into the ocean's mysterious depths, her heart singing to the rhythm of the sea. Intent on her thoughts, Josephine didn't hear the quiet young man approaching.

"Madam?" he said, touching her shoulder. "Are you all right?"

Startled, Josephine jumped and gasped.

"I'm so sorry to frighten you," he said. "It's going to be wild out there by the looks of it. The name's Gatlin, Quincy Gatlin. My friends call me Quince."

Josephine strained to see the young man's features, but shadows and a wide-brimmed felt hat hid his face from her.

"And you are?" he urged.

She thought for a moment. *Does shipboard etiquette vary from that of the drawing room,* she wondered. On land no gentleman would introduce himself to a woman. He'd arrange for a mutual friend or his host to make the introductions. Feeling slightly uncomfortable in the situation, Josephine swallowed, then introduced herself as Mrs. Josephine Van der Mere.

"Oh? Are you traveling with your husband?" the stranger asked.

She cast him a demure smile. "The rest of my entourage is suffering from mal de mer, I fear. I just stepped out of my cabin for a breath of fresh air."

"Ah, I see." The man leaned his elbows on the railing beside her. "It's a blustery night, isn't it?"

"To me, the sea is beautiful regardless of its mood," she whispered reverently. Even as she spoke the wind intensified and the waves grew larger. Large drops of rain pelted her face and cape. Within seconds, the raindrops intensified into a deluge.

"Come on, you're getting wet. You'll catch your death out here." Mr. Gatlin wrapped his arm about Josephine's shoulders and ran with her into the quiet dining area where the captain's first mate sat tending a cup of hot coffee. A flask of whiskey sat beside the man's coffee cup. A second man hunched over a table in the farthest corner caught her eye. *If I didn't know better* . . . The man in black had no way of knowing she'd board a ship for New Orleans. Yet by the hunch of his shoulders . . . A chill ran the length of her spine. Her first inclination was to confront the man with her suspicions. Fear warned her to be more cautious. If she were wrong, she'd be embarrassed. If she were right, he might do something violent.

Mr. Gatlin shook the rain off his greatcoat and hung it on a peg near the door. Then coming from behind her, he reached around her to untie her cape at the neck. Josephine's hands flew to the cords holding the cape in place. "I really should return to my quarters," she protested.

"One cup of hot coffee will get the chill out of those bones of yours," he argued as he managed to untie the cape and slip it from her shoulders. "How do you like your coffee, Mrs. Van der Mere?"

Uncomfortable with his presupposing manner, she whirled about and took the cape from his hands. "Thank you for the offer, Mr. Gatlin, but it's late and I'd rather return to my cabin before the worst of the storm hits."

As she spoke she could tell that the man in the corner was holding on to her every word.

Recognizing the uselessness of protest, Mr. Gatlin lifted his hands in surrender. "Yes, ma'am, whatever you say. By the way, give my regards to your husband."

"Likewise, give my regards to Mrs. Gatlin." With her cape slung over her arm, Josephine strode to the exit leading to the corridor and the private cabins.

Quincy Gatlin chuckled out loud. "There is no Mrs. Gatlin, Mrs. Van der Mere, at least the last time I looked."

With door in hand, she paused. "And there is no Mr. Van der Mere, Mr. Gatlin." She tipped her head respectfully toward the man. "Good night."

Her mind wrestled with the mystery of the man in black throughout the stormy night. As rain lashed against the sides of the ship, tossing it around like a cork in the angry surf, so Josephine's questions kept her spinning. When Annie crawled from her berth to be sick in the chamber pot at the foot of her bed, Josephine offered to help the girl. Annie protested. "There's not much you can do, ma'am."

"Here." She ran to her reticule and located a tin of candy peppermints. "This will help."

"Please, ma'am, I don't want anything but to feel better."

"Let me help you back to your bed and wash your face with cool water."

"And I'll only be sick again . . . ," the girl whimpered. "Please go to sleep, ma'am."

After helping Annie back to her bed, Josephine washed off Annie's perspiring face, then returned to her own bed. Thoughts of poor James below in steerage hounded her with Annie's every moan. *If only he could have slept in the servants' quarters,* she thought. *If only I'd left him home.*

The words to the Shepherd's Psalm came to mind. "He maketh me to lie down in green pastures: he leadeth me beside the still waters. . . ." Finally exhaustion won out and she fell asleep.

Morning dawned bright and beautiful. All traces of stormy weather was gone. The sun sparkled in the waves. Annie felt better as well. James, however, was still hanging over the side of the ship most of the time. He looked ghastly. "I don't think I'm going to make it, Mrs. Van der Mere. I think I'll die before I ever see land again."

"Let me move you to our cabin, at least during the day. And maybe by tonight, I can convince the captain to find you a space to sleep topside."

"No, no," he protested. "I'll stay right here. I have friends here." He introduced her to a family of five traveling to the gold fields of California. "And over there are two brothers from Prussia who are prospectors as well."

The people to whom he referred didn't look to be in much better condition than James. "Will you let me bring you a kettle of hot peppermint tea to settle your stomach?"

He agreed. Josephine made her way to the ship's galley, heated potable water in the kettle, and, despite the cook's protest, took the kettle and several mugs back to steerage.

After she'd comforted him as best she could and returned the tea kettle and mugs to the galley, she took a stroll on deck. She needed the fresh air. The stench of unwashed bodies and vomit had caused her stomach to do a few somersaults as well.

As she emerged from the darkness into the bright daylight, she cast her gaze upward toward the ship's slender masts. Men, with sisal ropes between their teeth, scrambled like monkeys up and down the masts.

She paused in the doorway to observe the drama, when out of the shadows a man's hand pushed her forward into a tangle of rope. It wasn't until later that she remembered catching a glimpse of a gold wristwatch, a rarity at a time when men preferred pocket watches and watch fobs.

Trying to catch herself, she managed to snag her right ankle in a smaller tangle of rope, rope attached to the yardarm. Josephine cried out in pain as the rope tightened around her ankle and yanked her off her feet. She landed like a sack of oatmeal on the deck. High up above her, unaware of her situation, a sailor swung the yardarm, dragging her, with skirts and feet flailing, across the wooden deck.

She screamed for help while wrestling to free her ankle from the rope, but the roar of the wind and the crashing of the waves against the side of the ship drowned out her cries. Another minute and she'd be swinging out over the water by one ankle and possibly falling to her death. The extra weight of Sam's treasure sewn into the linings of her crinolines and skirts made her struggle for freedom more difficult and would certainly drag her to the bottom of the ocean should she fall overboard.

From out of nowhere, a stranger clothed in black leaped to her aid. She caught the glint of a knife blade as he slashed the rope, setting her ankle free. Gasping for breath, she struggled to her feet. Before she could gather her wits about her, the mystery man was gone. For the rest of the day she looked for her rescuer, but he was nowhere to be found. At dinner, when all the cabin passengers gathered in the dining hall, the man was not there.

Everyone else on the ship, including the captain, had heard of her accident and voiced their concern over her safety. "A ship's deck can be a dangerous place," the captain warned, "especially for such a delicate flower as yourself."

She thanked him for his concern and promised to be more careful. She told no one about either the man who had pushed her or the one who had come to her rescue.

Quincy Gatlin insinuated himself at the table where Josephine and a Mrs. Castle, a dour matron of fifty, along with three older businessmen from Charleston, were seated. After coaxing her to retell her story, Mr. Gatlin said, "Obviously, Mrs. Van der Mere, you need a protector. I am electing myself to do so, at least until we dock in New Orleans where I disembark."

Josephine thanked him for his gallantry, then returned to the slice of boysenberry pie on the plate in front of her. She watched him out of the corner of her eye as he engaged the stony Mrs. Castle in conversation. His shock of reddish blond hair, sparkling blue eyes, and quick smile made him seem like a boy of fifteen while his wit and polish belied a man fifteen years older. *So engaging and charming,* Josephine thought. *A lot like Sam probably was as a younger man.*

Somewhere in the conversation Mr. Gatlin revealed that he'd been born in Atlanta and raised in Boston by a Harvard law professor and a literary mother. "She loves books," he explained. "Nothing makes her happier on a winter night than a roaring fire in the fireplace, a good book, and a bowl of MacIntosh apples."

Josephine admitted to herself that if it weren't for loving Sam, she could find Quincy Gatlin rather charming. Then she remembered Clare Thornton and wondered if such thoughts even mattered anymore.

When Mr. Gatlin suggested a stroll on deck, Josephine gladly accepted. The thought of returning for the night to the tiny cabin did not appeal. "I'll need to pick up my cape from my cabin and tell Annie where I'll be," she said. "I'll meet you on deck."

Mr. Gatlin started to say something, then stopped, smiled, and bowed. "As you wish."

Annie was curled up in bed, eating soda crackers and reading. Since her sea sickness lifted, she nibbled soda crackers around the clock. "I talked to James this evening," she explained. "He is still deathly ill. He wants to go home when we dock in Charleston, by train or coach, or anything other than by sea."

Josephine chuckled at Annie's humor, but the thought of James returning to Albany and the two women going on alone to New Orleans disturbed her.

"Annie, do you want to go home too?"

The girl shook her head. "No, ma'am, Mr. Sam needs us, he does."

Josephine gave her a hug. "Do you know how much I appreciate you, Annie?"

Annie grinned. "I sure do."

"Do you know how much I need you?"

Annie nodded. "I know that, too, Miss Josephine." Then her face darkened. "We are going on to New Orleans, aren't we?"

"I don't know, Annie. I just don't know."

Should she abandon the journey and return home? The greatest part of the journey, and the most dangerous, lay ahead of them. Should she stay in Charleston until Abe could come to their rescue? Josephine couldn't decide what was God's will. "A nice time to be asking yourself that question!" she mumbled while making her way to the dining room.

"I will be your protector." The words of Mr. Gatlin replayed in her mind. She'd assured the gentleman that his assistance would not be necessary, that she couldn't impose on his kindness. But now, here she was considering the protection of a complete stranger. What did she really know about him? And how could she explain her actions to Samuel?

She prayed for wisdom. "But Lord, Your answer must come quickly," she warned. "I have very little time to decide."

Later, after discussing the situation with Annie, Josephine had to make a decision. The ship was in port only long enough to unload goods from the factories up north. Besides, Sam needed her. She would go to him—or die trying, she decided. Besides, she and Annie wouldn't really be alone as long as Mr. Gatlin was watching over them.

With her decision made, Josephine bought tickets that would take James home to Albany on a series of trains. By the stack of tickets she handed him, she could tell that the poor lad would ride enough trains to last him a lifetime. "There are no direct routes," she explained.

"Ma'am, I surely don't mind as long as I don't have to put my foot on another boat!" he reiterated several times as she thanked him and saw him off at the railway station.

As Annie and Josephine's rented cabriolet made its way back to the ship, Annie tugged at Josephine's sleeve. "Miss Josephine, I could swear I saw the man in the carriage behind us on board the ship. I've seen him everywhere we've gone this afternoon, at the depot, at the livery, even aboard ship."

Josephine didn't bother glancing in the direction Annie had indicated. She knew the girl was right. She'd seen the man from the ship as well. And while it had been unsettling, she told herself that they would be safe under the protection of Mr. Gatlin. She had thought it strange that Mr. Quincy Gatlin couldn't go with them to the depot. He said he had business in Charleston. But he had arranged for the rented cabriolet and the driver to take them. *Oh well,* Josephine told herself, *I don't really intend to call on his help anyway, lest there be an emergency of some kind.* The man would just be an escort aboard ship, for propriety's sake, or if this man shadowing her every move should become dangerous. "I sure wish Abe was here," she said for the hundredth time.

~10~

Friend or Foe

THE *SEA WREN,* HER ROYALS UNFURLED, knifed her way through the windswept sea toward more southern waters with the precision of an Italian sculptor. Never before had ships stirred the hearts of seafarers and landlubbers alike as did the clipper ships Americans were producing. Josephine sensed the pride and the hyperbole of the magnificent vessel on which she rode. Long and lean, with sharp bows, raked masts, and a great cumulous sail, the ship was made for speed. She smiled to herself, thinking how much Peter, her husband, would have enjoyed these incredible beautiful ships. Soft winds playfully tangled the curls that escaped from the confines of her yellow-ribboned bonnet.

Josephine had forgotten she didn't stand alone at the railings until Quincy Gatlin's shoulder brushed against her sleeve as he spoke. "The state of Florida is a fairyland of enduring beauty. If you enjoy sun and sand and sea, you'll never want to leave." He slipped an uninvited hand onto Josephine's waist, then pointed toward the distant shoreline with his free hand. "Look, beyond the coral reef you can see palm trees. Aren't they beautiful? It is truly the land of the 'fountain of youth.'"

Josephine inhaled a deep breath of the fresh, clean ocean air and deftly eased out of the man's protective reach. "Fountain of youth? How fanciful, Mr. Gatlin. You're a poet."

"Quincy," he said, "call me Quincy. And yes, I can become quite poetic about the tropics."

Josephine dipped her head and batted her long eyelashes at him. "Mr. Gatlin, at dinner last evening you promised to tell me more about the swashbuckling pirates of the seventeenth century."

He chuckled as he drew her attention to a school of dolphins cavorting in the surf between them and shore. "They were a spicy lot, to be certain, and very much a part of the history of this area. Men like the infamous Blackbeard, Sir Francis Drake, and Admiral John Hawkins were probably the first Europeans to settle here. The sculpted coves and quiet inlets sheltered them from the open seas and curious eyes. Tales of lost treasures and fortunes are still told from here to the South American coast."

Josephine glanced up into Mr. Gatlin's face to find him transfixed by the magic of his own tale.

"Legend has it that a pirate named Normand lived on an uninhabited island near the little island of Tortola. Normand would lure ships into the coral reefs, then plunder them. One night he took a Spanish ship carrying so many chests of gold doubloons that he decided to bury them for safekeeping, along with the shipment of dye stuff and raw tobacco.

"Unfortunately Mr. Normand had a big mouth and bragged about his plunder. The authorities caught him and executed him before he could enjoy his ill-gotten gain. When the Tortolans learned of his execution, a group of them sneaked over to the island and dug up the dyes and the tobacco, but they never found the gold."

Josephine frowned. "Oh, that's too bad. So it's still there somewhere?"

Mr. Gatlin shrugged. "So they say."

"How thrilling!" Josephine shivered with excitement.

"Indeed it is," he continued. "I'd certainly love to find those chests of gold. Maybe one day."

"Mr. Gatlin, you are not driven by a lust for buried treasure, are you?"

He smiled at her, then turned his gaze toward the distant horizon. "My dear, Mrs. Van der Mere. There are two kinds of people in this world: those who have wealth and those who wish they did. I've always been one of those who wished. And some day, I intend to change that."

Josephine thought of the gold treasure she herself had sewn into all her skirts and crinolines. What would Mr. Gatlin think if he knew how much of a fortune she was wearing even as he spoke? Sam's gold and her own, along with bank notes and letters of credit, were enough to set up the enigmatic Mr. Gatlin for life.

"And, pray tell," she asked, "what ended the pirates' glory days?"

"The English got tired of them hassling their merchant ships, even though they were the ones who originally initiated pirating against Spain and Portugal. They didn't like it when the tables were turned on them."

Josephine laughed. "Sort of like teaching the American Indian to scalp the French during the French and Indian War."

He grinned down at her and nodded his head. "Another grisly plan gone awry. Of course, pirating might be a thing of the past, but smuggling thrives throughout the region to this day, that and transporting slaves from West Africa."

A shiver traversed Josephine's spine. His remarks hit too close to home. Slavery was no longer an event occurring in faraway places, but a reality of her everyday life now that she'd left the Northern states behind. Did Annie worry about that fact? Josephine's confidence wavered at the thought. As she glanced over Mr. Gatlin's shoulder, another shiver ran through her. The man dressed in black stood behind the stairs. She wondered if he was listening in on every conversation she'd had on board the ship.

Warm days and cool nights sailing around the peninsula of Florida passed quickly. Josephine took delight in frolicking porpoises that swam alongside their ship at times. The sleek creatures leaped from the water, their bodies shining with moisture. Schools of flying fish greeted them as they sped by. While the captain of the *Sea Wren* wasn't out to break any speed records on this journey, he didn't waste time loading and unloading cargo at many ports, so Annie and Josephine didn't stray far from the ship while in port. Sailing depended on the tides.

Nary a day passed but that Josephine didn't spot her mystery man lurking in the shadows. Fearful that Mr. Gatlin would take it upon himself to enter into a fisticuffs with the individual, she chose not to tell her ever-constant companion.

One day at the noon repast, the captain announced to the cabin passengers that they would be docking in New Orleans with the tide. "According to the charts, we'll be arriving at low tide so we will need to wait out the tide before we can dock."

Josephine and Annie spent the rest of the afternoon packing their clothing into their trunks, being certain that the heaviest of dresses were at the bottoms of the trunks.

"Just think," Annie gushed as she folded one of Josephine's gold coin-lined crinolines. "Tonight we will see Mr. Samuel." She cast a curious eye toward Josephine. "What do you think Mr. Pownell will think of Mr. Gatlin?"

Josephine reddened. "If you are implying what I think you are implying, you are wrong. Once I explained my position to Mr. Gatlin, he has been nothing but a perfect gentleman."

"I know it's not for me to say, but I don't like Mr. Gatlin." Annie tightened her lips and averted her eyes from Josephine's gaze.

A moment of anger flared in Josephine's mind, but quickly changed to laughter. "Annie, are you trying to protect Mr. Pownell's interests? Do you know that you are sounding more and more like Dory every day?"

"I didn't mean to. . . ."

Josephine dropped the chemise she'd been folding on the berth and hurried to Annie's side to give her a hug. "It's all right, Annie. I appreciate your loyalty. And yes, I still love Samuel Pownell with all my heart. Comparing Mr. Gatlin to Samuel is like comparing a sapling to a mighty oak. There is no comparison." A look of satisfaction swept across Annie's face as she returned to her task.

At dusk the two women rushed to the deck to watch the glorious sunset over the Gulf of Mexico along with the other passengers, both cabin and steerage, though the passengers from steerage stood apart from the rest. With Annie by her side, Josephine strolled closer to the clump of steerage passengers, mostly miners hoping to strike it rich in California. She noticed the look of hope they all shared, and the eagerness.

The harbor ahead was dotted with lights from the sailing ships that docked before the tide turned. And beyond the harbor were the city lights. Josephine was admiring the beauty of the evening when a smaller clipper ship sailed parallel with the *Sea Wren* and lowered her sails. Josephine watched the communication going back and forth between the two vessels. Not able to make out the name of the ship written on its bow, Josephine turned to the first mate who was standing nearby and asked about the ship.

"Oh, that's the *Russell Wright* out of Bristol, England," he said.

"England? My late husband and I talked about sailing to England one day."

"Would you like to meet the captain?"

"Indeed I would."

"Then come with me." He offered her his arm. "The captain and his first mate will be dining aboard the *Sea Wren,* and I know our captain would be honored to have you present."

Josephine pointed toward the small skiff rowing toward the *Sea Wren*. "Is that the captain now?"

"Yes, ma'am."

She smiled up into the first mate's weathered and jagged face. The man preened as he led her to the captain's dining room. For a man of five feet eight inches tall, walking next to a lovely blond woman of five feet two inches could make him feel like a giant among men.

Josephine had barely made herself comfortable in the captain's lounge when the two captains entered the room. A scruffy looking black child no older than seven or eight lingered near the door of the salon. When Josephine smiled at him, he dropped his gaze immediately. Her captain made the introductions.

"Mrs. Van der Mere is from New York," Captain Frazer informed the captain of the other ship. "Mrs. Van der Mere voiced to my first mate, Mr. Conklin, an interest in your country, Captain Benton. So I invited her to dine with us tonight."

Captain Benton bowed graciously, taking Josephine's hand in his and touching his lips to her fingers. "How gracious of you, Captain Frazer. After so many weeks at sea, a beautiful woman's company is a luxury I will enjoy."

Others of the more elite passengers were invited to join the dinner party. Josephine glanced around expecting to see Mr. Gatlin, but she decided that he hadn't been included in the captain's guest list.

After the six-course meal and the bread pudding for dessert, Captain Benton gestured toward the small boy who'd not moved from the doorway throughout the meal. "And now, I have another treat for you. Come, Tad," he ordered. "Play."

The child, his hands behind his back, inched closer to the table of dinner guests, his eyes luminous with fear.

"I said play something!" Captain Benton snarled.

The boy lifted a handmade pan flute to his lips and began to fill the small room with music, the music of the great European masters. When he finished the number, Josephine looked at Captain Benton and asked, "Where did he learn to play the music of the masters?"

"The slavers picked him up along the Ivory Coast. He speaks English as well, though I never have been able to pronounce his actual name so I call him Tad, short for tadpole. We suspect he was the houseboy of an English merchant."

"Slavers?" Josephine gasped. "He was kidnapped from his family?"

"Of course. The *Russell Wright* is a slave ship, madam. And my hold is full as we speak," Captain Benton growled, eyeing her suspiciously. "What are you, one of those abolitionists, Mrs. Van der Mere?"

Before she could answer, Captain Frazer shot her a disquieting look. "I am sure Mrs. Van der Mere is not an abolitionist, Captain Benton."

"Of course she's not. Pretty women like her don't think such dark and destructive thoughts, do they?" Captain Benton grinned her way, hoping to get a reaction from her.

Instead, Josephine patted her curls and cooed in her most delicate voice. "Oh, Captain Benton, you know us ladies so well. What with appointments with my milliner and with my seamstress, I hardly have time to tend to my tatting, let alone think about such awful subjects as slavery right here in our own country."

Captain Benton's face reddened, He turned to the child standing by the door. "Boy, play something else for us."

The child lifted the flute to his lips and played an early number by the gifted European, Chopin. Josephine tapped her fingers nervously on the table throughout the child's number. "Somehow, Captain, Chopin and slavery don't go well together, do they? What will become of the boy when we dock?"

"I expect to get a pretty price for him on the block. Don't go getting churchy with me, Mrs. Van der Mere. It's business, that's all. Besides, this kid will live a pampered life in some wealthy plantation owner's home or maybe in one of New Orlean's better bordellos."

The other women at the table gasped at the mention of a house of ill repute.

"Like a house pet," Josephine mumbled.

"Sorry ladies, I forgot myself for a minute," the captain explained. "My, that was good bread pudding, Captain Frazer. In fact, the entire meal was superb. I just might have to kidnap your cook."

The guests laughed at the man's little joke and moved on to other subjects. As the party was breaking up, Josephine took Captain Benton aside and asked, "I would like to purchase your musical genius."

The captain's eyebrows disappeared into his hair line. "He's going to bring a pretty penny, ma'am."

"In a few years, maybe. The fact that he's so young and will take special care will affect the price you'll be able to get," she argued.

The slave captain's eyes looked her up and down, coming to land on her steely blue eyes. "So what are you offering?"

"What do you want?"

"Gold. I won't take bank notes," the captain warned.

The two dickered for several minutes before settling on an amount. "All right, Captain, if you will give me time to go back to my cabin for a minute, I will have the gold coins for you."

The diners watched in surprise as the young widow exited the salon and returned shortly with a velvet pouch. Opening the drawstring, she dumped the coins onto the linen-covered table. A gasp passed through the onlookers as the coins rolled in every direction.

"Help me, you fool," Captain Benton shouted at his first mate as he hastily dived for the coins sparkling in the candlelight.

When he'd gathered them together and stashed them in the pockets of his jacket and his pants, the captain's first mate drew up a bill of sale for the boy which both the captain and Josephine signed. Captain Benton straightened. "He's all yours, madam."

"Thank you, sir." She cast the captain a wry smile. "But the child's not mine. He belongs to God." The man dropped his gaze to the floor.

Josephine made arrangements with Captain Frazer for the boy to stay in the servants' quarters. "I'll have my girl, Annie, stay with him so that he won't be afraid."

Word of the fancy widow's outrageous purchase and her gold flew through the crew and passengers aboard ship. Josephine led the boy to her stateroom to meet Annie. Annie was more than willing to care for the boy during the night. She gathered her clothing together and went with Josephine and the boy to the cramped space allotted her and the child in the servants' quarters.

Before leaving them for the night, Josephine explained to Tad what had happened. "I don't exactly know what I will do with you, but when you reach adulthood, you will be able to choose for yourself where you will go and what you will do. Do you understand?"

Hiding behind the folds of Annie's skirts, the boy nodded to the blond lady. He'd never seen such light colored hair before. "What did you say your name was?" she asked.

The child mumbled a name that sounded as if it included every letter of the alphabet. When he saw a look of bewilderment on her face, he broke into a shy smile. "Call me Tad."

Josephine chuckled and tweeked the boy's cheek. "Well, Tad, you stay here with Annie and I'll see you in the morning."

The decks were empty by the time Josephine hurried back to her stateroom. Only the night watch was about. As she opened the door to her cabin, a folded note that had been stuffed in the crack fell to the floor. She reached down and picked it up.

"Beware! Pirates still abound today." She glanced about, but no one was in sight. She stepped inside her room and instantly knew someone had been there since she left to take Annie and the boy to the servants' quarters. She looked around but couldn't find anything missing. She opened her trunks and felt her skirts. The gold was all there. She checked the lining of her cape. The letters of introduction and bank notes were all accounted for as well.

The man in black! Thankful the journey would be over in the morning and she would be safe in Sam's care, she undressed quickly and knelt beside her berth. "Heavenly Father, I know I can trust in You. I know You will keep me from harm. 'Yea, though I walk through the valley . . .'" With the promise fresh on her lips, she hopped into bed. In the velvet darkness of her cabin, she recited the words of Psalm 91. She fell asleep in the promises of her Father's love.

~*11*~

Reunion Day

THE GENTLE ROCKING OF THE SHIP, ALONG with the promises of God she'd claimed and trusted, lulled Josephine into a deep sleep. She awoke with a start to the calls of deckhands outside busy putting the ship to port. The sun was high in the morning sky. Josephine couldn't believe she'd slept so late. There was so much to do before they docked at the wharves of New Orleans. "Annie!" Josephine bolted from her berth. "Where's Annie?" Annie never slept beyond sunrise. Usually Josephine had to shoo her away in order to catch a few extra winks.

Josephine hastily threw on the clothing she'd laid out the night before and stuffed her nightwear into her portmanteau. One last glance about the cabin assured her that she was leaving nothing behind. She knew the ship's porter would be by soon to take her trunks ashore.

Grabbing her portmanteau and doeskin reticule, she dashed from the room and down the corridor toward the servants' quarters. "Annie! Annie! Wake up! We are really late this morning. The ship is already dock—"

She swept the curtain back that divided Annie's space from the others' and stopped midsentence. "Annie? Tad?" The area looked swept clean—no Tad, no Annie, and none of her belongings could be seen. "What in the—"

"Breakfast. Probably the child was hungry and she took him to the servants' salon to eat." Following up on her hunch, Josephine hurried through the ship's corridor to the servants' eating area expecting to find Annie and Tad hunched over a bowl of porridge and hard bread. But no, no one was in the salon either.

"On deck! That's where they are—on deck watching the ship dock. Of course!" Josephine took a deep breath and smiled. "What little boy wouldn't find the workings of this grand ship fascinating?"

With more speed than grace, Josephine stepped out of the ship's interior into the brilliant Louisiana sunlight. She blinked from the pain of the glare.

The wharves of New Orleans resounded with the clamor of commerce. Deckhands' backs glistened from the sweat of hard labor, their shouts to the longshoremen mingling with the cries of sea gulls and the bustle of early morning life.

Josephine paused along the railing long enough to view the sailing ships stretching out of sight along the waterfront. Trading ships, fishing boats, schooners of every hue and size, a few nondescript vessels she could only wonder about lined the wharf where they were either being unloaded or scrubbed down by deckhands.

The *Sea Wren*'s propulsion on the high seas hung limp, her masts brushing the clear morning sky. On shore a few elderly men paused to admire the ship's beautiful lines, or at least that's how Josephine read their expressions.

Remembering her purpose, the woman moved through the crowd of passengers lining the railings, with trunks and cases, cloth bundles and wooden boxes piled high by their sides, waiting to disembark.

"Annie? Have you seen my maid, Annie?" She asked first one person then another. Spotting a shiphand sitting on a pile of rope, repairing a tear in one of the canvas sails, she asked him, "Have you seen a colored woman and boy out here this morning?"

"No, ma'am," he answered. "But people have been disembarking for the last hour or so, some left the ship as soon as we docked. Maybe your girl was among them."

"No! That's ridiculous. Annie would never go anywhere without checking with me first," Josephine protested.

The deckhand smiled at what he saw as the woman's naiveté. Obviously she had a runaway on her hands but wasn't smart enough to know it.

"It's not what you think." Josephine tried to explain. "Annie is my friend as well as my personal maid. She would never—"

"The captain. You need to report your loss to the captain." He returned to his sewing.

Frustrated, Josephine stood in the middle of the milieu not knowing which way to turn. She hoped to see the familiar face of Quincy Gatlin, the man who vowed to be her protector. Perhaps he'd know what to do. But, alas, he was not to be found either. She couldn't even find the mysterious man in black when she needed him.

"Madam, you look bewildered? May I be of service?" The first mate tapped Josephine on the shoulder and smiled down in her worried face.

"You certainly can!" She explained about her missing servant and the young boy she'd purchased the night before. "Something bad has happened to them, I know it. Annie would never just walk away without telling me."

The first mate gazed at her, nodding as she spoke, and

responding to her agitation with a contrastingly cool demeanor. "Madam, often owners think they know these black folk, but there's no telling what they might take in their minds to do. Like children, you have to watch them all the time."

Josephine glared at the man. "Will you please conduct a search of the ship. I know something's very wrong here."

The first mate bowed gracefully. "Of course, madam. And would you like your luggage unloaded in the meantime?"

"Yes . . . yes, please." Obvious to her, the man didn't recognize the emergent nature of the situation. Her anxiety rose with the air temperatures. For late fall, the sun grew intensively hotter than normal as she paced the decks.

When the captain learned of Josephine's loss, he ordered a stem-to-stern search of the vessel, but first he ordered Josephine to "stay put" on deck while his men conducted the search.

"I won't have you wandering into dangerous areas of the ship or tripping over ropes," he added, a twinkle evident in his eyes.

Josephine fumed as she watched the captain walk away. She flung her hands into the air in disgust. "Stay put! He says to stay put! I have one little accident during the cruise and he treats me like a clumsy child. And that wasn't my fault either!"

After more than an hour, Captain Frazer reported that neither the boy nor Josephine's maid were aboard ship. "I would recommend that you go to your final destination, madam, then report them missing to one of the agencies that handle such problems. There have been so many runaways in the last few years, the plantation owners hereabouts have organized an agency to retrieve their runaways for them—bounty hunters, I think they're called."

Josephine shivered at the mention of the term. "But, Captain, I know Annie and the boy didn't run away. I'm afraid something much darker, much more evil has befallen them."

The man smiled and patted the agitated woman's arm. "Now, my dear, I know you're upset, but—"

Josephine's face hardened. Jutting her tightened jaw, she gazed at the man through slitted eyes. "Thank you, Captain, for your advice. If you will excuse me, I need to go ashore and hire a rental cab to take me to my destination."

He bowed graciously. With all the dignity she could muster, Josephine picked up her two bags, turned on her heel, and marched down the gangway onto the dock.

Her eyes stung with tears. "I don't know where to start looking for transportation to Miss Clare Thornton's home. "Cypress Lane. Lord, where is Cypress Lane? I need some help here."

She'd walked half the length of the towering *Sea Wren* when she realized she noticed a familiar figure leaning against a stack of empty cotton crates. She was almost upset enough to walk directly over to the man in black and ask him for his help finding Cypress Lane.

The cacophony of the busy seaport roared around her. The cries of vendors selling their wares, longshoremen unloading cargo, harried travelers greeting family and friends, and merchants shouting orders at slow-moving workers filled the morning air.

She considered her option as she stepped off the wharf and onto the cobblestone street parallel to the waterfront. Seeing what looked to be a carriage driver leaning against a beat-up carriage, she turned toward him to ask him about acquiring land transportation when, above the din, she heard someone call her name.

"Mrs. Van der Mere! Mrs. Van der Mere!" Josephine turned in the direction of the call. It was Quincy Gatlin waving at her from across the busy street. "Over here. I have a carriage waiting for you. Over here!"

He ran to her aid, immediately taking her bags from her. "Let me get you situated in the brougham before I locate a boy to stash your trunks in the carriage's boot." Mr. Gatlin gestured to the driver. "See that the lady's made comfortable while I locate her luggage."

For the first time in what seemed like hours Josephine felt safe. "That's more than I can say for poor Annie," she mumbled as the driver took her hand to help her into the vehicle.

"Josephine! Josephine!" Despite all the noise, she heard her name called again, but this time by a voice she once thought she'd never hear again. It was Sam calling. Tears sprang to her eyes as she swung about on the carriage step to locate the source of the voice. Through a mist of emotion, she spotted the face of her beloved coming to her through the crowd. All her composure melted at the sight of his strong, smiling face.

"Samuel! Samuel!" Josephine leaped from the carriage step into the surging crowd. When she did she lost sight of him. "Is the entire world taller than I?" she sputtered, moving blindly in Samuel's general direction.

As she pushed her way past two slower moving pedestrians, Josephine came face to face with Samuel Pownell. In an instant, he swept her into his arms and whirled her about in a circle. "My beautiful one. I can't believe my eyes."

"Nor can I. Oh, Samuel, I've missed you so much," she cried, her arms tightly wrapped around his neck, her feet dangling ten inches from the ground. "How did you find me?"

His warm and tender brown eyes stared deeply into hers. "An associate alerted me to your arrival, but that's not important right now. Josephine Van der Mere, you are so beautiful. I've missed you so much."

Her heart melted at his words. She reveled in the warmth from his strong, gentle arms. That she'd ever doubted the endurance of his love, she couldn't imagine. For an instant he stared into her eyes, then shifted his gaze to her lips. Breathless with anticipation, she closed her eyes. Slowly, deliberately, despite the gawking crowds, he placed his lips on hers. For Josephine, the world stopped. All thoughts of Annie and Tad, all anxiety regarding Clare Thornton disappeared.

As their lips separated, applause broke out from the passersby who had seen the tender kiss. Embarrassed, Sam lowered Josephine to her feet. Josephine buried her face in his gray silk vest.

"Josephine, darling. It feels so right having you in my arms once again. I can't wait to introduce you to Clare. Where's your luggage? Did you travel here alone?" he asked incredulously.

"No, of course not. I'm—" How could she explain that she'd sent James home because of illness and somehow lost Annie?

"Well, well. And who might this be?" Quincy Gatlin strolled up to Josephine, a sly smirk on his face. His grin darkened to a glower as his eyes connected with Sam's. "Obviously you two are on a first-name basis."

Sam shot a glare toward Josephine. "Who is this man?" he asked.

Josephine blushed. "Samuel, let me introduce you to Mr. Quincy Gatlin. Mr. Gatlin has acted as my protector after I had to send James back to Albany. Annie and I couldn't very well travel such a distance without someone to watch over us, now could we?"

"Oh really now. Then I suppose I owe you a word of thanks," Sam extended a hand toward Gatlin.

Quincy took it. "It was a pleasure, sir. No trouble at all, I assure you."

"And just what is your business in New Orleans? Or are you here on pleasure?"

Gatlin looked uncomfortable. "It's been a pleasure, sir, up to this point."

Sam's face darkened. "I'm sure it has. By the way, you mentioned Annie. Is she with the luggage?"

"Annie! Oh, no. I can't believe I forgot her in the excitement. The most terrible thing has happened, Sam. Annie has disappeared. When I went to find her this morning she was gone from her sleeping quarters, she and the boy."

"The boy?" Sam asked.

"Yes, last night aboard ship, I purchased a seven-year-old boy from a slave trader. I know it was a stupid thing to do, but I couldn't let him be fed into this heinous system!"

Sam squinted down at her. "And you say they are both gone?"

"The captain searched the ship for me. No one saw them leave. I have no idea where they could be."

Somewhere in her telling the story, Quincy Gatlin uttered surprise at all that happened. At the right moment, he interrupted. "I am so sorry for your loss, ma'am, but if you'll not be needing my service further, I must be going."

"She won't, I assure you," Sam growled.

Josephine smiled up into the man's face. "You have been so kind, Mr. Gatlin. Thank you again for everything. And may God go with you." She extended her hand to him.

He bowed and kissed the back of her fingers. "It has been my pleasure."

"Will we be seeing you again during your stay in New Orleans?" she asked, as Sam slipped his arm possessively about her waist.

Gatlin cast a quick glance toward Sam's expressionless face. "Only God knows." He bowed and headed for the waiting carriage.

"I have a carriage waiting. And I've sent a man to pick up your luggage." Sam placed Josephine's hand in the crook of his arm and started walking down a side street lined with brightly decorated stalls. "The first thing we need to do is get you back to Clare's place, then I can begin the search for Annie and this boy of yours."

"I am so sorry for all of this. Are you mad at me for disobeying your instructions and coming myself instead of sending Abe?"

Sam glanced down at her and patted her hand. "Are you kidding? You're much more pleasant to look at than Abe, as good a friend as he is."

"But I wasn't completely honest with him. I told him you wanted me to come to you instead of him."

Sam threw back his head and laughed. "I know. He sent a telegram telling me which ship you were on."

Oh, God, how beautiful, she thought seeing and hearing Sam's beautiful laughter once again. "That reminds me," she said. "I promised to telegraph Abe and Dory to let them know we arrived safely."

"It's right over here," Sam replied. As they walked toward the telegraph office, Josephine inched closer to his side as they walked, hardly believing she was here, in New Orleans, walking beside her beloved Sam.

After they sent their telegram, Sam oversaw the loading of the trunks onto the rented buckboard, then climbed into the open air carriage where Josephine waited. Both had been concerned that none of the luggage be found missing.

When they finally climbed aboard the waiting coach, Josephine settled back against Sam's shoulder. She could barely contain her joy at being with him once more. "I must write Serenity again, to make sure she knows you are alive. She never responded to my letter and I'm afraid the letter was lost."

"I'm so grateful that you've written her," Sam replied. "I have had to be so careful to keep a low profile. I was afraid even a letter might be intercepted by the authorities."

Suddenly Josephine sat bolt upright. "Oh, I almost forgot to tell you. Your daughter Serenity is engaged to marry Caleb Cunard."

A satisfied smile swept across Sam's face as he closed his eyes against the bright New Orleans' sun. "Ah, that's nice."

She glanced at him in surprise. "That's nice? Is that all you have to say about your daughter's engagement?"

Sam chuckled aloud. "I knew my daughter would have enough sense to fall in love with the Cunard boy. He'll make a gem of a husband for her. She'll never starve while in his care."

"How romantic!" She folded her arms across her chest and tapped her gloved fingers impatiently. "Men!"

He laughed again, then drew her into his arms. "Romance? You want romance?" He kissed her neck and ear. Noticing the smiling faces of passersby, she wriggled to free herself from his grasp.

"Sam! Stop it," she hissed. "We're in public, remember?"

He held on to her. "Ummm! I love the smell of your perfume."

"Well, I can certainly see that you've regained your strength after your injuries!" she huffed, trying her best to act like a prim New England lady.

"All right." Sam laughed. "I'll be good."

As they rode toward the outskirts of the city, Josephine told Sam about her scheme of hiding their fortune in the linings of her skirts and crinolines.

"Do you mean you're wearing a king's ransom right now?" he asked.

She fluffed her skirts and grinned. "That's right."

"And I thought you'd just put on a little weight since I saw you last."

Indignant she cuffed his arm. "Of all the—"

"You were mighty heavy back there when I swung you into my arms."

"Hmmph! Did you ever consider that you might still be weak from your debilitation?"

His shoulders shook with laughter. "I deserved that one."

Folding her arms across her chest, she turned her face from him. "Yes, you certainly did."

"Wait until you meet Clare. She's one remarkable woman. I can't understand what's wrong with the men in this region. She'd make someone a mighty fine wife."

"As long as she's not yours," Josephine sniffed.

"Mine?" Sam looked at her in astonishment. "You thought that I might be—"

"Well," she defended, "your letters were certainly vague about the future of our relationship and about your feelings for me, hardly the missives of a man in love."

"I am sorry for that. I told myself it was for your protection, but in some ways, it was to protect my heart. Everything happened so fast in Auburn last summer. We'd been engaged such a short time and I didn't know if you felt the same for me as I—"

Josephine placed her hands on her hips and glared. "Do you think I give away my affections to the first handsome man who glances my way?"

Suddenly, the carriage hit a rut tossing Josephine into Sam's startled arms. At the same time, her bonnet slipped from her hair onto her shoulders. Her golden curls cascaded to her shoulders. She struggled to recapture the errant curls. Sam caught her hands in his, then tenderly brushed one of the stray locks from her cheek. "Your hair is like spun gold. You are so beautiful. If we were alone . . ." He glanced toward the carriage driver then back at her. ". . . I would shower you with kisses until all your doubts regarding my love for you were washed away."

Her heart pounded as she lifted her face to his and leaned toward him. Instead of the expected kiss on the lips, she felt his lips press against her forehead. "Not here; not now. Our day will come, my sweet. I promise. Our day will come."

~12~

The Unveiling

 THE STACK OF GOLD GREW IN THE MIDDLE OF Clare Thornton's oak table as the two women unraveled the stitches concealing Sam's and Josephine's personal treasures. Two empty gunnysacks lay under the highly polished table, waiting to be filled. The ladies chatted as if they'd known each other for years, while Sam paced the floor, tabulating the bank notes he'd uncovered from beneath the trunks' linings.

"Mr. Cox didn't want to turn over your money to me." Josephine laughed, remembering the look of distrust on the weak-chinned attorney's face the day she brought Sam's letter into his law office. The solicitor had been Sam's partner and confidante before Sam ran for state assembly and had moved to Albany at Sam's suggestion. "Your brother tried to gain control of your assets in Albany, but Mr. Cox refused. He cited a little-known law on the state's books that stated Cox had the right to hold a man's assets for one year before turning everything over to his heirs. He decided to use that year to locate Serenity before giving the money to your brother."

Sam laughed. "Good for Willy." He waved the bank notes as a fan in front of his face. "I knew I could count on him. But tell me, how did you manage to convince him to turn everything over to you?"

"I didn't, or at least he didn't trust me with everything of yours. He's still holding half your assets. He says he'll send them to you through the banking system where you eventually settle. But it was your letter that made him cooperate as far as he did. I think he was so relieved you were still alive."

Josephine smiled at the retired schoolteacher sitting across the table from her. "Thanks to you, I might add. I don't know how to thank you."

Sixty-year-old Clare Thornton, as lean and as angular as an ironing board but with a smile that could light a concert hall, nodded, her eyes twinkling with happiness. "Just take good care of my boy." She glanced up at Sam, who smiled as he excused himself to help unload the carriage.

As Josephine looked around the woman's parlor, she noted how it matched the woman herself. Simple, sparse, and possessing a natural grace, the room measured a scant twelve-foot square. White lace curtains fluttering in the breeze from the open windows softened the absence of a carpet on the dark wood paneled flooring, polished to a shine. A floral tapestry covered sofa and two side chairs with upholstered seats played second fiddle to the focal point of the room—a rosewood pianoforte. On the wall behind the pianoforte was mounted a violin and a well-used bow. Josephine ran her fingers over several keys of the pianoforte. Crisp clear tones echoed off the room's high ceiling.

"Do you play?" Clare stood in the doorway to the dining room. She was carrying two ice-cold glasses of lemonade.

Josephine shook her head. "I always wished I could, but no, I'm afraid not."

Clare handed one of the tumblers to Josephine. "It was my father's. He was a concert musician."

"Really?" Josephine touched the keys reverently. "I had a friend who—"

"Charity Pownell?"

Josephine opened her mouth to reply, but bit her lower lip instead and nodded.

"Charity must have been an incredible woman. I've heard so much about her," Clare admitted.

Josephine's eyes misted. "She was." She lifted her gaze toward the narrow staircase where Sam and the carriage driver were wrestling the first of Josephine's two trunks. "Sometimes I wonder how he can love me, after her."

A broad smile rearranged the lines on the older woman's face. "Ah, but he does, and that is what matters. Believe me, he talked about you as well."

Josephine sipped the cool, refreshing liquid. "Thank you for being so nice."

"And truthful! Never forget that." The woman took a sip from her glass as well. "I wouldn't flatter you about something as important as Sam's love. If only I were twenty years younger . . ." A twinkle teased the corners of her eyes. "You may try to play the instrument if you like."

Josephine shook her head but continued to trail her fingers along the music rest. "The boy that I told you about? He is quite the musician. Tad can coax the most lilting melodies from his hand-carved flute. Some of the tunes I recognized as European."

"Really?"

Josephine sensed Clare's reaction wasn't due to idle curiosity. "From my limited knowledge of music and musicians, I'd say the child's a genius."

Clare asked several questions. Josephine tried to answer each of them. Then during a lull, Josephine asked, "Tell me about Sam."

The woman chuckled as she gestured for Josephine to join her on the sofa. "I've praised the Lord every day since He brought Samuel to my door. Without his expertise, my friends and I would have been caught by the bounty hunters. He taught us how to run a rail station more efficiently. And Samuel used his own funds to move the cargo from here, north." She sputtered in protest, "I didn't ask him to do that."

When Sam returned, Josephine anxiously asked if he'd found Annie. Sam frowned and pursed his lips. "I have several men out looking for her. But New Orleans is a big place, and unless God intercedes, a black woman and child could easily be swallowed up by the city."

"No, I can't accept that!" Josephine slammed a gold coin down on the table, rose to her feet, wadded the skirt she'd been working on, and tossed it to the floor. "Annie trusted me. I've let her down." Suddenly, Josephine stopped, scowled, then turned to Sam. "What did you say?"

"I said New Orleans is a big—"

"No, not that part. The part about God interceding."

Sam looked at Clare, then back at Josephine. "I think I said it will take an act of God to—"

Josephine's eyes brightened. She shot him a wide grin. "That's what I thought you said. Was that a figure of speech or do you mean what you said?"

Sam looked baffled. "I-I-I meant what I said."

"But you," Josephine continued, "always said religion and trust in God is nothing more than a pretty fable and a way for con men to steal one's money."

Sam took a deep breath, took her hand, and led her back to the table. "Sit down. I can see there's a lot about me you need to understand. Yes, I used to say those things and believe them, but three months captive to Miss Clare Thornton can change any man. Every day, whether or not I was conscious, dear Clare read the Word of God to me, hour after hour. And, well, last month I attended her church for a revival service and gave my heart to God in an altar call. Two weeks ago I was baptized."

"Baptized?" Josephine looked first in one face, then the other. "I've never even been baptized."

Clare's grin widened. "I'm sure Reverend Brock will be glad to change that."

Tears glistened in Josephine's eyes as she touched Sam's face with her fingertips. "I can't believe it. Even in my wildest imagination, I never would have believed such a thing could happen. Your disbelief was the only flaw in an otherwise perfect husband-to-be."

Sam blushed. "Be my wife for fifty-plus years, and I'm sure you'll uncover a few more chinks in my armor." He leaned down and kissed her on the forehead. "Let's get back to tabulating this money and determining which is yours and which is mine."

Josephine smiled wryly. "But we're engaged, Samuel."

"Yes," he assured her. "And when we're married, we can combine our assets, but for now, it's important to be circumspect about our finances."

Across the table, Clare looked up from her raveling. "Samuel, I feel the need to stop what we're doing and pray for your Annie."

A stab of fear shot through Josephine's heart. Sam nodded his head and dropped into the dark oak chair at the end of the table. "I think that's a good idea, Clare. I trust your premonitions."

Clare took Josephine's hand with her left hand and Sam's with her right. Shyly, Sam and Josephine linked hands as well, forming a circle. They bowed their heads and Clare began to pray.

"Heavenly Father, Thou hast promised to be with Thy children through the storms, through the fire, and through the valley of death. Thou has said Thee would never leave, nor forsake us. Annie is one of Thy children, Lord. I don't need to remind Thee. Bring her home safely to us. And, this young child, Tad, so far from home, help him to be brave and help Annie to be at peace, resting in Thine everlasting arms. Amen."

Sam cleared his throat to begin his prayer when the front door of the cottage flew open. Before Sam could leap to his feet, Peter Van der Mere III and two rough, desperate-looking men burst into the room. Instantly their eyes lit upon the stacks of gold. Their faces broke into greedy smiles. "My, my, what have we here? See, fellas, what did I tell you?"

"Peter!" Josephine gasped. "How did you . . . ? What are you doing here?"

Sam tried to leap to his feet only to have the man nearest him wave his pistol in Sam's face. "Peter? You know this man?"

Van der Mere threw back his head and laughed. "Did you really think you could run from me, Mother dearest?"

"Mother?" Sam gasped. "What is he talking about?"

"Tell him, Mommy dear. Tell him how you cheated me out of my rightful inheritance," Peter chortled, brandishing his weapon under her nose.

Josephine arched a defiant eyebrow and pushed the pistol away from her face with her hand. "It seems my late husband, Peter Van der Mere . . . ," she explained for Clare's benefit, ". . . had a son by his first wife. Before we married, my late husband sent him to Europe to live with his aunt since dear Peter could do nothing with the lad. At that time Peter gave his son his share of the family fortune." She gazed up at Peter. "How am I doing?"

"Fine, so far," the young man sneered.

"My husband's will stipulated that his son could never receive another cent from the estate. Peter's aunt had sent word that the boy had gone through his inheritance at the Parisian gaming tables in less than a year. And . . . ," she paused for effect, ". . . the will stipulated that if I should, in sympathy for the boy, give him more of his father's wealth, I would lose my inheritance as well."

"Very good! Very good!" Peter applauded. "And now, it looks like I'm going to just take the money that's coming to me." He cast a sly glance at Sam's steel-hardened face. "And I'll get a bonus, so it seems, Assemblyman Pownell. You are Assemblyman Pownell, I presume. The man ousted from his elected office in the state of New York for breaking the laws he'd sworn to uphold?"

"Aren't you the pot calling the kettle black, young man?" Clare demanded. "Barging uninvited into my home and brandishing pistols in our faces, then threatening to steal these people's money?"

Peter stared at the older woman in surprise. From the nearby windows, late afternoon streaks of sunlight slanted across Clare's weathered face.

"Who is this woman? Where did you find a feisty old hen like her?"

"You have no respect for anyone, do you?" Josephine defended.

"Why should I? What's she to me?" Waving his pistol in disregard for his hostages, Peter stode across the room. He pushed back one of the lace window curtains and peered out into the gathering shadows. "You expecting anyone, Pownell?" he asked.

"Yes, in fact, I am," Sam admitted. "An armed posse."

Peter whipped his head around to face Sam. "Then you'd better pray that posse doesn't show up, if you want to come out of this alive."

"Personally," Clare interjected. "I have better things about which to pray, son."

"Shut up, old woman!" He swung his arm back as if to strike Clare. Sam started to his feet only to be dragged back down in the chair by the beefier of Peter's companions-in-crime.

Returning his attention to Sam, Peter said, "I considered turning you in for the reward, Pownell. That's why we're here, but this is better." He gestured toward the stacks of gold coins. "We get the money without bringing the law into the transaction. Me and the law, we don't always see eye to eye."

Josephine scowled. "But, Peter, how did you know I was coming to New Orleans? I told no one."

Peter laughed again. "I had you followed, you foolish little pigeon. When I learned you were on the *Sea Wren*, I bought passage on the next ship out of New York City. We docked mere hours after the *Wren*."

"Ah," Josephine exclaimed to Sam. "That explains the mystery man, the man in black."

"Mystery man? What mystery man?" Sam shot a surprised look at Josephine. "You didn't tell me about any mystery man."

Josephine shrugged her shoulders. "I haven't had a chance, what with Annie missing and all." Sam fell silent as Josephine told about the months she'd spent worrying over the stalker. "He was always dressed in black and he sported a full black beard. A couple of days before I left Albany, Abe tried to catch him and managed to reinjure his leg in the process."

"This mystery man of yours wears all black?" Sam asked.

"What are you babbling about? She said he did, didn't she?" Peter interrupted. "I don't know anything about your mysterious stalker. Quincy doesn't wear black! He's a peacock when it comes to fashion."

"Quincy?" Sam and Josephine shouted simultaneously.

"Yeah, Jake, go tell Quince to get in here." Peter strutted back to the table. "I hired him up north to shadow you, Step-mommy. What a stroke of genius to have him befriend you along the way, then to kidnap your maid last night."

"Why?" Josephine threw her hands in the air. "Why Annie?"

Acting as if he were explaining the world to a six-year-old, Peter said, "We were going to hold her for ransom, but now that I have the king's ransom, we'll just sell her and that kid to the highest bidder."

At the sound of approaching footsteps, Josephine turned to see a red-faced Quincy Gatlin. He had a shotgun slung over his left shoulder.

"Hello, Mrs. Van der Mere," Quincy mumbled, avoiding her gaze.

"Quincy? Quincy Gatlin?" Josephine's words caught in her throat. Tears glistened in her eyes, along with anger. "I trusted you. . . ."

Peter grunted. "That'll teach ya to trust every yokel you meet."

"I'm sorry, Mrs. Van der Mere. I'm the one who broke into your cabin while you were dining with the captain." Quincy's face deepened to an uncomfortable magenta. "I truly am sorry."

"You were the one who broke into my cabin?" she asked. "What were you looking for?"

"Whatever gold was left after you bought that slave kid. But I didn't find anything." His gaze shifted to the skirts discarded on the floor. "I never thought to look there, in your clothing."

"You never thought! You never thought! Such incompetence," Peter snorted. "I'm surrounded by idiots!"

Sam's face darkened with rage. He snarled at Josephine. "You didn't tell me about anyone breaking into your cabin."

She was about to respond when a glint suddenly caught the corner of her eye. She turned to see a flash of gold as Quincy nervously ran his fingers through his hair. He wore a gold watch on his wrist.

"The watch!" Josephine exclaimed, suddenly remembering seeing it the night she was pushed into the ropes aboard the clipper. Quincy quickly interrupted her, continuing his confession. "Yes, I'm the one who pushed you the first night of the voyage. If it hadn't been for the arrival of that stranger, whoever he was, I would now have your blood on my hands. I've never killed anyone, honest."

Josephine gasped. "You would have killed me?"

"That was the plan," Peter interjected. "Your death would leave no one to challenge my right to contest my father's will. But then, Quincy here got cold feet and I had to modify my plans."

Quincy Gatlin shot a look of hatred toward Peter, then

gazed at Josephine tenderly. "Once I came to know you, I realized I could never hurt you."

Josephine's eyes spat fire at the strangely repentant young man. "You don't think it hurt me when you kidnapped one of my best friends, Annie?"

"I'm sorry," Gatlin dropped his gaze once more. "God forgive me for what I've done."

"He'll have to, because I can't!" Josephine snapped.

"He can and will forgive you, Mr. Gatlin." Everyone turned in surprise toward Clare. In a quiet, controlled voice, she explained, "God died so that your sins could be forgiven, Mr. Gatlin. He promises that if we confess our sins, He is just to forgive those sins. God loves you, Mr. Gatlin, despite all you've done."

A burst of laughter erupted from Peter. "Him? God loves him? Old Quince sold his soul to the devil many years ago, didn't ya, Quince?"

Clare disarmed everyone by adding, "And Jesus Christ bought it back again, Mr. Van der Mere. Yours too, in fact. He shed His blood so that you and I can be forgiven and live eternally."

Like a fox stalking its kill, Peter moved closer to where Clare sat. "Lady, you've got a lot of nerve! I could put a bullet in your brain, just like that." He leveled his pistol at Clare's forehead.

Sam and Josephine gasped, steeling themselves against the expected explosion, but Clare maintained a steady stare deep into the aggressor's eyes. "Only if God so ordains. You and all the powers of hell cannot stand against the King of the Universe, Mr. Van der Mere!"

Peter turned to Sam and asked incredulously, "Who is this crazy old biddy?" Peter's scorn set Josephine's teeth on edge. She longed to leap to her feet and scratch that self-important sneer off his face. Silently counting to ten, she stared past Clare to the lace curtain billowing in the afternoon breeze.

Out of the corner of her eye, Josephine saw Quincy finger the trigger on his shotgun and slowly level it in Peter's general direction. "Leave the lady alone, Peter. We're here for the gold, remember? Let's take the money and leave."

Peter pushed the barrel of the shotgun aside. "Never point that thing at me again unless you intend to use it, Gatlin!" Peter snarled. "And it would take more of a man than you'll ever be to use it on me! All right, fellas, grab those potato sacks under the table and fill them with the gold coins."

The other two men greedily scooped up the coins and stuffed them into the two sacks.

"Tie the bags off," Peter ordered. While Peter watched one of the men secure the top of the one gunnysack, the other on Peter's right dropped a single gold coin into his shirt pocket.

Peter's arm was swift. The barrel of his pistol caught the man on the cheek, knocking him to the floor. Blood gushed from the man's face.

Peter bent down and ripped the coin from his companion's hand, stuffing it into his own vest pocket. Showing no sign of emotion, Quincy hauled a gray cotton handkerchief from his pocket and tossed it to his injured companion.

Ignoring the interaction between his two cronies, Peter snatched the sheaf bank notes from Sam's hands. "I'll take those as well." He smirked as he stuffed them into his jacket pockets.

Grabbing the bulging gunnysacks under his arms while continuing to aim his pistol at Josephine's head, Peter ordered Quincy Gatlin and the other two men to go for the horses. As Quincy turned to leave, Clare called out to Quincy, "I will be praying for your soul, Mr. Gatlin."

Before Peter could respond, Clare raised her calm, steely gaze to his face. "And yours, too, young man."

A momentary flash of fear appeared in Peter's eyes, then was quickly replaced by a look of derision. He grabbed the bags of gold, one under each arm and laughed. "Nice knowing you folks. Lady," he directed his remarks at Clare, "you can thank that God of yours for sparing your lives today, unless you, Mr. Pownell, try to follow me. If you do, I'll cut you down faster than a skunk on a log."

Sam's jaw tightened. He was barely controlling his rage. Josephine sent him a warning "he's not worth it" look. Sam leaned back against his chair, continuing to gaze defiantly into Peter's eyes. Peter fingered his pistol as he took a step closer to Sam, then without warning, he turned and dashed out the front door of the cottage.

Peter's feet had barely thundered across the parlor floor when Sam leaped to his feet and charged after him, kicking over his chair in the process.

"No, Sam!" Josephine cried, grabbing his arm as he darted past her. "It's not worth it. He's not worth it." Furious, he tried to yank his arm free of her grasp, but she refused to let go.

At the same instant, Clare flew around the end of the table and grabbed his other arm. "She's right, Samuel," she pled. "Let God take care of Mr. Van der Mere."

"But the gold!" He tried to shake off the two women's stubborn grip.

"It's only gold!" Clare shouted into the man's ear. Her words startled him out of his rage. As the muscles in Sam's arms relaxed, a grin spread across Josephine's face. He shot her an irritated look, but it didn't stop her. She giggled, than laughed. Sam and Clare stared at her as if she'd taken leave of her senses.

"What? Whatever is so funny?" Sam growled, shaking free from Josephine's hold on his arm. Shaking free from Clare's hold took more effort. "Do you think losing our entire fortune is a cause for laughter, woman?"

"No," Josephine gulped between bouts of laughter, "but think for a minute. Your friend Mr. Cox didn't know how much of a favor he would be doing you holding half of your fortune back in Albany. You can't imagine how hard I tried to convince him to give it all to me."

The three of them fell quiet at the sound of galloping horses fading into the distance. "They're gone, praise God." Clare pounded her fist decisively on the oak tabletop. "That is exactly what we need to do—praise God and then pray for each one of them." It was now Josephine's turn to stare in surprise. The woman left her speechless. Josephine's heartbeat had barely returned to normal, and this now-retired schoolmarm was offering to pray for the filthy varmits.

"Haven't you read in God's Word about the importance of giving thanks in all things?" Clare nodded her head emphatically as she spoke. "Besides, we need to pray for that Quincy boy. He wants to do right; I know he does."

"Quincy? We should pray for that bounder?" Josephine couldn't believe the woman's words. "I'd rather bring down the curses of heaven on his head."

"I can't blame you," Clare chuckled. "But he has a soul. And that soul is in conflict tonight with the demons of hell. God isn't through with Quincy Gatlin yet. That boy needs our prayers."

Sam shook his head in wonder. "You are a fearsome warrior, Miss Clare."

The woman grinned again. "If God be for us, who can come against us? And now's the time to go to battle against the enemy. It's time to call in the big guns!"

Clare took each of their hands and physically dragged both Sam and Josephine into the parlor. "Come on. This is one of the times in your life when your faithfulness can be put to the test. We'll begin by giving thanks to God for all that's happened. For this is the direct will of God. You do want to do His will, don't you?" She eyed Josephine patiently.

"Yes, but—"

"Then we forgive our wayward brothers."

"Forgive . . ." Josephine shook her head in defiance.

The woman cocked her head to one side and cast Josephine a devilish grin. "Do you think the good Lord didn't include you in His prayer when He told the disciples to forgive as they'd been forgiven? Do you think Quincy Gatlin's crime against you is worse than the ones perpetrated against Jesus Christ on the cross when He said, 'Father, forgive them'?"

". . . for they know not what they do." Sam flexed and unflexed the muscles in his jaw. "You're right, Clare. As usual, you're right."

The battle raged within Josephine's heart as she watched Clare kneel down beside her horsehair sofa and saw Sam join her. *This is the man I fell in love with?* Josephine asked herself. *And I was praying for his soul all these months. Maybe he should have been praying for mine.* Reluctantly, Josephine dropped to her knees and bowed her head.

~13~
Mysteries Revealed

"Before they call, I will answer. . . ." Clare arose from her knees. The woman ignored the doubt-filled glances exchanged by Josephine and Sam. "That's what God said, simple as that. Now, is anyone hungry for supper? I have a basket of fresh vegetables I brought in from the garden this morning. And if my suspicions are right, Ed will be by in a few minutes with his catch of the day and I'll mix up a great gumbo. Have you ever had gumbo, Mrs. Van der Mere?"

"Josephine," Josephine urged. "Please, call me Josephine."

Sam extended his hand to assist Josephine to her feet. "Or Josie, as I like to call her."

Josephine cast her fiancé a sidewise grin.

The rumble of a buckboard drew Sam's attention to the front window. He pulled back the lace curtain. "Uh, I think it's time I cleared up a little misunderstanding." He gestured toward the sofa.

"Who's out there, Samuel?" Clare moved to a second window. "I don't recognize the man, do you?"

"Actually, yes, I do. And I think Josephine might also recognize him."

Impelled by curiosity, Josephine peered around Sam's shoulder at the tall, full-bearded stranger stepping down from the buckboard. A black felt cowboy hat shaded the eyes of the man, but she recognized him instantly by his stance. "It's him, the man in black!"

"Oh, dear . . ." Sam reddened and scratched his closely trimmed beard. "I believe I am the one responsible for your mystery man, Josephine."

"You?" She watched the stranger drape the reigns around the hitching post. A familiar bolt of fear skittered up her spine to her brain. His wasn't the kind of face a frightened woman would soon forget. He wasn't darkly handsome like Samuel. He had a tough demeanor that spoke of danger.

Sam strode over to the door. "Yes. I hired Jeff Coombs to watch over you, Josephine—protect you, if you will. I didn't mean for him to frighten you, just watch over you in my absence."

"Frighten me?" Josephine gasped. "I was paralyzed with fear. I thought he was a bounty hunter trying to catch Abe or me breaking the law. Why didn't you tell me about him?"

Sam hurried to her side, kneeling on the floor in front of her. He took her reluctant hand in his. "I apologize. I knew you wouldn't like it and neither would Abe, but with the price on my head, I didn't know what my enemies might do."

Josephine snatched her hand away from Sam. "I can't believe you would do such a thing and not tell me." Through the window she could see the tall, rangy stranger amble up the front pathway toward the cottage.

"If I told you, would you have cooperated with him?" Sam demanded. "Be honest."

"I don't know!" Josephine folded her arms across her stomach and glared. "Probably—"

"Probably not!" Sam finished her sentence. He rose to his feet and opened the door before the man had a chance to knock.

"Jeff, good to see you, friend." Sam stuck out his hand and drew the man into the parlor. "Let me introduce you. You know my fiancé, of course, but she hasn't had the pleasure of meeting you, has she? Josephine, say hello to Jeff Coombs." The man removed his wide-brimmed felt hat and mumbled a greeting.

Josephine politely extended her hand, but the surly expression on her face gave away her true feelings.

"And this is my very dear friend, Miss Clare Thornton," Sam explained, glaring at Josephine behind Coombs's back.

Clare knew no strangers. "Welcome to my home, Mr. Coombs." The man had barely removed his hat when she asked, "Have you eaten?" The stranger shook his head.

"Oh, bosh, I know you haven't. I can always tell." She gave him a broad smile. "You're welcome to stay. I'm just about to begin making supper."

Jeff Coombs swept his gaze about the neat and simply furnished parlor. He shot a pleading glance at Sam, as if asking for permission to accept her offer.

"We'd love to have you stay, Jeff," Sam volunteered. "Besides, you and I have a lot to talk about."

Jeff smiled shyly at the older woman. "Er, yes ma'am, that would be very nice."

Josephine lifted her nose in the air as she sized up the man she'd found so frightening for so long. Her voice was low and feminine. "So you're the man who has been terrorizing me for the last few months."

He ducked his head and blushed. "I guess so, ma'am. I ain't too good a spy, am I?"

Sam shifted the conversation and asked, "So, Jeff, what have you and the other men learned about my young maid and the little boy under her care?"

"Excuse me," Clare started toward the hallway leading to the kitchen. "Josephine, I could use your help out here, paring the vegetables for the gumbo."

As she strode from the room, Josephine wondered when was the last time she'd been ordered to help pare vegetables. For the first time, Clare Thornton reminded Josephine of her own mother.

Clare moved about the kitchen with a smooth gait, lighting oil lamps and drawing water from the indoor pump. "I tried to tell Sam that you had ten thousand angels watching over you without complicating things by sending this Mr. Coombs to New York, but he wouldn't listen. He loves you so much."

She handed Josephine a paring knife and a basket of freshly picked vegetables. "Here you go. I think we'll need everything, if Mr. Coombs is as hungry as I suspect."

"Uh-huh," Josephine mumbled. She wondered what the last few months had been like in the little cottage on Cypress Lane. She imagined Clare and Sam had had some pretty heated discussions, yet as she watched the interplay there was no doubt that they both had enormous respect for each other.

Clare stepped out the back door and returned with a string of catfish. "Great catch! I'll scale them out on the back porch."

Glancing out the window at the twilight, Josephine's thoughts turned to Annie. How frightened she must be! How alone! "Dear God," she breathed, "be with Annie right now. Give her courage. And lead the men to her soon."

Josephine was so intent with her paring and her praying that she didn't hear Sam walk into the room. "Jeff and I are heading to the waterfront. That's where he told the other men we'd meet them."

"Oh, Sam, do you think you should go there?" Concern flooding Josephine's face. The knife in her hand trembled. "What if someone recognizes you? You're a wanted man, remember?"

He looked past her with calculated indifference. "Can't be helped. Tell Clare we'll be back for supper as soon as possible, hopefully with Annie and the boy." A kiss to the top of her head and he was gone. She closed her eyes and listened as the buckboard rumbled toward town.

When Clare shooed Josephine out of the kitchen to rest, Josephine made writing a new letter to Serenity her first task. She'd been so relieved to find Sam in as good health as he was, even with his obvious limp. Yet she could tell that his injuries had taken a lot out of him. She could see a lingering pain in his eyes. She told Serenity what she could and promised to write more later.

The delicious aromas from Clare's stew simmering on the stove enticed Josephine back to the kitchen.

After Clare made her finishing touches to the fresh gumbo, the ladies decided to go ahead and eat rather than wait for the menfolk. Revitalized by a delicious supper and a short nap, Josephine slowly surveyed the delicately appointed guest room. Simple and uncluttered, the room had soothed her jangled nerves the moment she stepped inside. White-washed walls, pale lavender and white gingham Priscilla curtains, and a white cotton bedspread embroidered with blue and lavender forget-me-nots welcomed her.

Upon waking, she changed into a blue calico dress with

crocheted edging circling the round neckline. It was the only lightweight gown she'd brought with her that wasn't made of hard-to-care-for silk. Making her way down the narrow stairs, she looked about for her hostess, but the place was empty.

"Where can she be?" Josephine glanced beyond the parlor's sparkling windowpanes. A full moon played hide-and-seek with the branches of a nearby cottonwood tree. Her mind flashed images of potential disaster for people she loved. She strode to the front door and stepped out onto the small wooden porch. A breeze whispered in the trees above her head and tousled her hair about her shoulders. Her ears responded to the unaccustomed sounds of the bayou. She took a deep, steadying breath. The aroma of burning leaves filled her nostrils.

"I will not fret. Worry does absolutely no good," she announced to a hooting owl nesting in a nearby tree.

Josephine heard the familiar hymn before she saw Clare come round the edge of the porch. She smiled to herself as the older woman sang the words of courage. "God is the refuge of His saints, when storms of sharp distress invade. . . ."

Turning her thoughts toward Sam, Josephine's face softened. She remembered his angular, softly bearded face and the deep bronze of his skin since living in the South. The ridge of callus on his hands was new as well, probably from cutting wood for Clare. She remembered the tender look in his eyes when she first saw him at the wharf. She grew heady with emotion thinking about the pressure of his arms around her waist and his lips pressed against hers. She'd never known such pleasurable feelings before.

The sound of footsteps came from behind the cottage. A withered, bone-thin black man of fifty or so came around the corner of the house. Clare stopped singing in the middle of a verse. "Ed! You're back again. I have some gumbo on the stove if you're hungry."

Spotting Josephine, the man went rigid with suspicion. "Where's Mr. Sam?"

"He's in town looking for the girl." A sweep of Clare's hand and Josephine was included in the circle. "You haven't met Mrs. Van der Mere yet, have you?"

"I gotta find Mr. Sam!" The man's expression sharpened. "I's know where her stepson is, and the girl, and the gold. They's at The Bloody Nail, gamblin' away Mr. Sam's money."

"Are you sure?" The screech in Josephine's voice startled both Clare and the man called Ed. "Take me to them!"

The man's face darkened. "I don't think so, ma'am. It's not the place for a lady."

"Nonsense!" Whirling about with determination, Clare marched up the steps to the porch. The wind whipped her skirts about her ankles. "Get over to your place and hitch up your cart. We're going to town." She waved her hand toward Josephine. "Come on, don't just stand there. We need to grab our bonnets. We have no time to waste."

The women impatiently waited on the front steps until they heard the creak of Ed's cart wheels and the clop of his swayback mare. They leaped to their feet and rushed at the cart.

"I don't like this." Ed shook his head as he helped the women into the back of the wagon. "I don't like this at all."

One small lantern in the seat beside Ed lit the narrow path through the cottonwoods. Conversation between the women was impossible as the wagon bounced over the ruts. Josephine hung onto her hat with one hand and gripped the shaky wooden slats of the cart with her other hand.

Suddenly they saw another buckboard racing toward them. They rounded a corner and there it was, encroaching on their side of the narrow lane.

"Whoa, girl!" Ed shouted and yanked on the reins, swerving into the ditch and sending his passengers topsy-turvy. The women screamed as they landed in a heap in the long grass beside the road. The lantern tumbled off the buckboard set and into the grass as well. Fortunately the damp evening dew prevented it from catching flame.

The driver of the other rig brought his horses to a stop, then ran back to where the upended cart landed. In the darkness, he extended his hand to Josephine. She allowed him to help her to her feet. When she went to thank him, she gasped. "Quincy!"

"Mrs. Van der Mere? What are you doing out here?"

"I should be asking you that question."

"Oh, yes, wait a minute." He darted for his buckboard. She heard him shout, "Annie, you can come out now! You're safe."

Annie? Josephine's mind couldn't comprehend what was happening until she felt Annie's trembling arms around her. "Oh, Annie, you're safe! Praise God, you're safe."

Rushing to the buckboard, Clare didn't wait for an invitation. She scooped the frightened Tad into her arms. "Here, child. You're safe now, child."

Quincy Gatlin stepped up behind Josephine, rolling and unrolling his felt hat in his hands. He spoke in an embarrassed whisper. "Ma'am, I am so sorry for the pain I've caused you."

She looked at him for a long measured second. "Why did you bring them back?"

He cleared his throat. "It was what Miss Thornton said,

that she was praying for me. Nobody ever prayed for me. I know you said you couldn't forgive me, but I did ask God to. That's why I had to bring them back to you before more people got hurt."

Josephine swept her gaze over the sobbing girl in her arms. "Annie? Are you all right? Did anyone hurt you?"

"No, not too much, Miss Josephine." Sobs erupted from Annie's throat.

Pain stabbed at Josephine's heart. "I am so glad you're safe. You're the closest to a family that I've got. I don't want anything to happen to you." She turned her attention to Quincy. "I have to thank you for bringing her home to me, Mr. Gatlin. The fact that you rescued her and Tad from my stepson, Peter, will go a long way toward my forgiving you."

"Thank you." The darkness hid Gatlin's features. It was only by his voice that she could tell he was overcome with emotions.

"Ed," Josephine heard Clare call. "You have to find Sam and bring him home. He and his men headed toward the waterfront."

"I'll help you," Quincy shouted, running toward his buckboard. "Let's take my rig. We'll get there faster." As he stopped to help Ed on board, he tossed a filled gunnysack off the side of the wagon. The bag landed at Josephine's feet. "Here. I managed to save some of your money before Peter lost it all at the poker table."

Annie spoke up. "Mr. Peter made Tad play his flute for the men in the bar. When Tad played the hymn 'Amazing Grace,' the owner of the bar ordered Peter to get us out of his establishment. That's when Mr. Gatlin rescued us." Annie's eyes reflected the strain she'd been under during her ordeal. "Mr. Peter had planned to sell Tad to the owner and use me for poker ante if he ran out of gold."

Caressing the back of the girl's soft, curly head with her free hand and rocking her back and forth with her other, Josephine cooed soft assuring words into Annie's ear, like a mother comforting a young child.

Seeing Clare leading Tad back up the road toward the cottage, Josephine whispered to Annie, "Come on, let's go home."

"Home?" The longing in Annie's voice broke Josephine's heart. She didn't need to ask the young woman how homesick she felt, nor could she fault her. Annie had endured far beyond anything either of them ever suspected she would. "To Miss Thornton's home for now, Annie. You'll be safe there."

Several hours later, after helping Clare heat bath water for both Annie and Tad, Josephine sprawled unladylike on the parlor sofa. "I'm exhausted. That was hard work," she commented to her companion. "I wonder when the men will get home? Sam will be relieved to learn that more than half of our gold was in that bag, along with most of the bank notes. As if that's important now . . ."

Clare looked up from the book she was reading, a pair of round, wire-rimmed spectacles perched on the end of her nose. "Patience, Josephine. Sam will return in good time."

"Hopefully in one piece," she muttered. To deflect further comment, Josephine changed the subject. "What are you reading?"

"A Greek tragedy called *Antigone*."

"You enjoy that stuff?" Josephine screwed up her face in distaste.

"No, not really." This wasn't the answer Josephine expected. Clare removed her glasses with one hand. "I read it whenever I need to take my mind off other things. It takes all my concentration, you see."

Josephine's laugh brought a grin to Clare's face. "And here I thought I was the only one worried about what was happening tonight."

Clare knitted her brow. "Not exactly. I believe worry is not only a killer, but a sin. So, rather than fuss about things I cannot control, I praise God for His promises of protection, then focus my mind on other things. In this case, *Antigone* by Sophocles."

Restless, Josephine rose to her feet, grabbed a knitted shawl from the back of the sofa, and ambled out onto the porch. She strolled along the dirt road toward town, then turned back toward the cottage after a few yards. The threat of a wandering alligator or two kept her within a short run to the modest clapboard cottage at the edge of the swamp.

Throughout the remainder of the night, she found herself floundering in the spirit-debilitating land of anxiety. She made feeble attempts to praise God as Clare had said, but before she even realized it, her thoughts returned to the vain imaginings of a frantic woman. "Lord, I'm trying. You know I am trying."

Exhausted, she curled up on the porch, while inside Clare softly played melodies from an old Yankee hymnal Josephine had earlier seen laying on the top of the pianoforte. Comfort and peace seeped into her muscles and into her soul.

-14-

A Humble
Proposal

IN THE GRAY LIGHT THAT PRECEDES THE breaking of morn, Josephine awoke to the sound of approaching vehicles. Her muscles ached as she struggled to her feet to see Quincy and Sam perched side by side on the buckboard leading a procession of wagons. A second buckboard followed, driven by Jeff with Ed by his side. Six swarthy looking men on horseback brought up the rear.

Josephine bounded off the porch and into Sam's waiting arms. Quincy climbed down from the buckboard as Josephine and Sam murmured sweet snippets of love to one another. The cottage's screen door slammed and Clare strode out onto the porch. "You're back, Mr. Gatlin. I knew you'd be back. God isn't finished with you yet. And where's the other one—Peter Van der Mere?"

Sam straightened and shot a quick glance toward Quincy. "He's dead, Clare. The man's dead."

The tragic words hung in the cool moist morning air like long johns hanging on a clothesline during a rainstorm. "Dead?" Josephine paled and covered her mouth with her hand. "Did you . . . ?" She couldn't bring herself to ask the question both she and Clare were thinking.

"No, we didn't shoot him, if that's what you want to know, though I would have if it had been necessary," Sam protested, his gaze one of decision and determination.

"Oh, I'm so relieved." Josephine melted into his arms.

"Then who did?" Ambling down the steps, Clare strode purposefully toward Quincy, her eyes burning into his soul.

"Not me, ma'am." He threw up his hands in protest. "Old Peter was already dead when I got to the casino with Sam and his men."

"Then what happened?" she demanded, standing chin to chin with the former bandit. "Who killed the poor young man?"

"Poor young man?" Josephine snapped. "He stole our money. He was going to kill me."

"But he didn't, so tell me who killed him?"

With his arm around Josephine's waist, Sam replied, "Peter Van der Mere III was killed by a fellow gambler for hiding aces up his sleeve. Shot to death while holding enough of a treasure to last him a decade or more."

Clare turned her gaze once again to Quincy. "Is that how it happened, young man?"

"Yes, ma'am! Honest! I left the casino with the girl and the child when the arguing broke out. I had no idea Peter would get shot. He was winning."

Satisfied with his answer, Clare rounded up the men, promising them hot grits and soda biscuits with gravy once they washed up at the well in back of the cottage. "Come on, Josephine, let's feed these fellas. They must be hungry as bears by now."

By the time Annie and Tad stumbled down the stairs, the men had beached themselves in the parlor. Clare hurried to reheat the grits for Annie and Tad, while Josephine dried the last of the breakfast dishes. "Done just in time to start again." She placed her hands on her back and stretched.

Clare placed her iron skillet on the flame to whip up another batch of gravy. "That's the anthem for today's woman."

Josephine paused, her cheeks flushed with high color and good health. "Yes, I guess it is."

"Some women object," Clare shrugged, "but for a single woman like me, I find it exhilarating to serve others, especially when I can see they're enjoying my efforts."

Josephine thought about the woman's words as she hung the cotton dishtowel on a metal hook by the back door. Having been the daughter of a cook, she'd washed her share of dirty dishes. When Peter Van der Mere II came along and freed her from such labor, she thanked her lucky stars. She glanced down at her red hands, wrinkled by water, and smiled. *After all the efforts on Charity's part to turn me into a lady, I am back where I started, washing dishes.*

She'd barely admitted to herself that somehow she didn't mind, when Sam strode into the kitchen and over to where she stood. "The men have left, all except Quincy. He wants to speak with Clare."

Their lives settled down somewhat during the month that followed. The season changed from autumn to winter, as much as seasons change in Louisiana. Both Sam and Tad thrived in the mild temperatures of the South. Josephine could see Sam growing stronger. His limp became less pronounced and the strain she'd noted in his eyes when she first arrived disappeared.

For a time after her abduction Annie had nightmares. With the presence of the peaceful and confident Clare, Josephine began to see Annie's natural exuberance for life returning.

Clare's example of faith and trust in God permeated her little home and everyone in it. Once, soon after Josephine and the others arrived in New Orleans, Sam suggested that it might be easier if he and the others found a place of their own. While Clare only replied, "If that's what you want," she pouted the rest of the day. By supper, even Sam, who seldom noticed people's moods, realized that Clare's feelings had been hurt, that their presence brought her as much happiness as her home gave them. He did insist that he pick up the cost of food for the household.

Christmas Day brought a flurry of activity at the tiny cottage. Tad and Clare worked up a special Mozart presentation as their gift to everyone. Annie constructed a manger scene out of gingerbread as her gift for the occasion. She also made a batch of Sam's favorite oatmeal cookies.

Josephine convinced Sam to take her shopping in New Orleans one day while he was taking care of business there. She found a white silk, Spanish lace shawl for Clare and a box of seven monogrammed linen handkerchiefs, embroidered with flowers and edged with three-inch crocheted lace. For Tad, she purchased a biography on the lives of famous musicians. Since Clare had taught him to read, the child's appetite for the written word was voracious. For Clare's friend, Ed, and for Quincy, who'd been spending a lot of time at the cottage, Josephine purchased pairs of fine camel-brown leather gloves.

When it came to Sam, she knew exactly what she wanted, expensive or not. In a small bookstore along New Orleans' main downtown area, she found a leather bound black Bible. After purchasing it, she took it to a nearby jewelers to have it engraved. When the engraver finished, he handed the book to her. She looked at it and sighed. She'd been tempted to put Mr. and Mrs. before the Samuel Pownell, but decided that might not be wise. She didn't doubt he loved her, but there'd been little mention of marriage since she arrived in New Orleans. In a cottage as small as Clare's, their privacy was at a premium. Someone was always around.

Celebrating Christmas morning surrounded by family and friends, Josephine knew she'd never had a more perfect holiday. Her gifts for everyone couldn't have been more perfect.

Sam gave her a gold watch pendant. As she gazed at the delicate etchings of forget-me-nots on the cover, for a moment she saddened. Quickly she hid her disappointment for the gift. Imported from Holland, it couldn't have been more exquisite. Yet Josephine had been hoping for an engagement gift, something to indicate that their romance would move on to the next logical step. The woman couldn't help but wonder what was hindering Sam making a formal commitment. After all, they'd announced their intentions to Serenity back in upstate New York before their lives took so many different turns.

Josephine also knew that Sam, Ed, and Quincy were secretive about something. One or all of them would be gone for as long as a week at a time. She suspected that the men were building a strong Underground Railroad unit in the area. Though concerned over Sam's welfare, Josephine felt a strange relief from the stress of clandestine meetings and dangerous liaisons. She knew that Annie appreciated the calm as well. And with so many people living at Clare's place, especially young Tad, the retired schoolteacher had dropped out of the system.

January and February passed quickly. They received the

news of Serenity's wedding to Caleb with rejoicing. Secretly Josephine wished she could have been at the wedding. Sam and she agreed that Serenity and Caleb's idea for an inn where travelers could rest before facing the wilds of American's western territories sounded exciting. She did have her doubts about the young couple living in a sod house with dirt floors. In her worst poverty, she'd never had to endure such deprivation. When she voiced her doubts to Sam, he reminded her that if Caleb and Serenity loved one another as much as it seemed in her letter, a dirt floor or sod walls wouldn't be a problem.

One midday at the beginning of March, Sam came into the kitchen just as Josephine was drying the last lunch dish. It was quiet, and perfect weather for wearing a shawl. Annie had gone to the room the two women shared to do her mending, while Clare and Tad had retired to the parlor to practice his reading. Josephine winced as Sam caught her rough red hands in his and brought them to his lips. Gone were the smooth porcelain-like hands of days past.

In a husky voice, he said, "Let's take a walk together. We have a lot to talk about."

Josephine blushed. Her pleasure at his touch made her feel giddy. She'd forgotten the others watching the romantic interlude and let him lead her into the warm sunlight.

They strolled hand in hand down the dirt road without speaking. Words didn't seem necessary after all that had happened. Josephine's heart sang an anthem of joy and thanksgiving with every step.

"You know how much I treasure you, don't you?" he began. "More than life itself."

"And I you, Samuel."

Pausing to face her, he took a deep breath as if waiting

for a wave of unexpected emotions to subside within him and tilted her face up toward his. "Enough to abandon your New York lifestyle for the frontier existence in Independence, Missouri, or say, the California gold fields?"

He touched her lips as she started to reply. "Wait. Don't be hasty. This is important. I know that I proposed once before but so much has happened since that could have changed your mind."

"Changed my mind?" Josephine stared at him in disbelief.

He touched a finger to her lips to silence her. "For me, there is nothing in New York. And beyond the price on my head here in Louisiana, things are likely to be heating up for me in these parts."

"What do you mean, heating up?"

"I'm sure you know what Ed, Quincy, and I have been doing." She nodded slowly. "Well," he continued, "we have managed to set into motion five spurs to the Railroad in these parts alone. But one of our connections has been compromised. Fortunately, only my name was revealed."

"Sam! No!" Panic filled her heart. To lose him again? She couldn't handle the thought.

"Sh, sh. It's all right for now." He stroked her upper arms as he spoke. "Quincy and Ed will be able to manage the other four after I leave."

"Sam, I won't let you—"

"Honey, stop. Listen to me. I'm not out here to discuss the problems of the Underground Railroad, I'm here to ask you to marry me. Serenity is the only family I have, outside of my avaricious brother in Buffalo. So I want you to think long and hard about your answer."

She opened her lips and inhaled as if to speak. He stopped her. "Think, darling, think. You're a young woman.

There are hundreds of men, wealthy men, who would give you a life of luxury and parties."

She tried to reply again and he touched her lips a third time. This time she swatted his hand away from her lips. "Will you stop doing that? Let me speak! You are an old fool, Mr. Pownell, if you think I am looking for wealth and prestige. I love you!" She spat the words in his face. "Can't you see that? I love you!"

Josephine swung around and started back down the road toward the cottage, sputtering in anger with her every step.

"Josephine!" Sam raced after her, flailing his hands as he tried to explain. Without warning she skidded to a stop and whirled to face him. Her boots danced with irritation and her eyes snapped. "That has to be the most unromantic proposal any woman ever received. Of course, I'm going with you to Missouri, or California, or any other place on the face of the earth! Was there ever any question?" She waved an index finger in his stunned face. "Don't think I will let you weasel out of your commitment to me, not after I traveled halfway around the world to reach you. Cold feet or not, you're stuck with me, Mr. Pownell!"

A quirky smile teased the corners of his mouth as she sputtered on about the necessity of his honoring his commitments. "As to the house in Albany, I've had two buyers approach me in the last six months. I'm sure Mr. Cox—"

Suddenly it was her turn to be surprised. Without warning, she felt Sam scoop her into his arms and his lips crush against hers. Sometime during the kiss, she encircled his neck with her arms. When he withdrew his lips from hers, she leaned forward, desiring a second kiss. Instead he whispered in a husky voice, "Will you marry me, Josephine Van der Mere, today?"

~15~

New Beginnings

"TODAY?" HER EYES BLINKED OPEN. SHE gasped and stared at him.

"Today, before I change my mind."

Fury flared in her eyes. She pummeled his chest. "Let me down. I demand you let me down!"

Sam threw back his head with laughter as she squirmed in his arms. His laughter and her angry shouts brought Clare and Quincy out of the cottage. Annie and Tad came running around the corner of the house as well. Josephine was still kicking and squirming in Sam's arms when they appeared around the bend in the road.

"Whatever are you doing to that poor girl?" Clare demanded.

"I'm marrying her, that's what. We going to have a wedding today!" he announced, setting Josephine unceremoniously on her feet once more. "Quincy, I won't press kidnapping charges against you, nor theft, if you'll be my best man." With a twinkle in his eye, he grinned at Clare. "And there's no doubt who will be second-best lady at this shindig."

"Samuel," Clare sputtered, "you can't expect a lady to prepare for such an important event as her wedding on such short notice!"

Josephine trailed her finger tantalizingly along Sam's bearded cheek, then sent a devilish grin toward the older woman. "Oh, yes he can."

Encircling Josephine's waist with his hands, Sam swung her around and around. Her skirts billowed as they twirled like young children in the tangle of grass.

Clare clicked her tongue and headed for the house. "Quincy, turn left at the fork and you'll see a community church just past the grove of oak trees. Warn Pastor Bleau that he has a wedding to perform. We'll be there in a couple of hours. Come on, Annie. I need your help with the sewing. Someone around here has to have some sense!"

As she started for the house with Annie in tow, Tad tugged at her skirts. "What will I do, Miss Clare?"

"You will play the music, of course, the number you played for me a few minutes ago. And I need you to pick a bouquet of flowers as well."

Noticing the baffled look on Tad's face, she scolded, "Didn't you hear me, young man? Get a move on."

His hand automatically shot to his forehead. "Yes, ma'am."

"And you, Sam," Clare called from the front porch. "You go change into your Sunday-go-to-meeting duds. And do something about that scraggly beard of yours!"

Sam laughed and saluted the determined woman. He knew better than to tangle with Clare Thornton while the woman was on one of her missions. In Josephine's ear, he whispered, "Guess I'd better obey her before she takes a cat-o'-nine to my tail."

Josephine leaned into his kiss, dreading the moment she could no longer feel the warmth of his hands on her waist.

"Soon, darling, soon. You will be my wife and we will

spend the rest of our lives holding one another." His voice broke with emotion.

"Till death do us part." A bittersweet smile formed on Josephine's face as she mumbled the familiar words on the way back to the cottage. At the top of the stairs, Sam kissed her lightly on the lips and aimed her toward the sounds coming from Clare's bedroom. "Until later, my sweet. Until later."

***

Josephine lived through the next couple of hours in a daze as Annie and Clare poked and prodded and fitted a delicate lavender chambray gown of Clare's to Josephine's tiny body. When she protested to Clare that the gown had never been worn and had cost the woman much too much, the older woman waved away her objections. The woman ignored Josephine when she suggested that the lace-edged square neckline needed to be higher. With a hassle of pins in her mouth, Clare sputtered, "You're down South now, my dear, not in the priggish North."

In no time at all, Quincy's buckboard was outside the cottage to take the ladies to the chapel. A proud and dapper Quincy helped the bride onto the padded leather driver's bench. The others climbed onto the wagon for the short ride to the chapel.

Upon arriving at the little church, Clare scooted down from the wagon before Quincy could round the vehicle to help her. Annie and Tad ran after her. Josephine took Quincy's gloved hand and allowed him to help her from the wagon. As she gazed at the tiny, white clapboard chapel, a soft smile touched her lips. She'd wanted a wedding in a church when she married her sea captain, but the irascible Peter Van der Mere had other plans. Without fanfare and ceremony, he arranged for one of his sea captain friends to officiate on deck of a rolling cutter. After the ceremony, he'd taken her home to his summer place along the Hudson River.

As Josephine climbed the front steps of the chapel on Quincy's arm, she could hear the wheezing pump organ begin to play. The lilting notes from Tad's flute followed. She didn't recognize the song but she knew it was appropriate to the occasion. Quincy opened the door to the church foyer and Josephine stepped inside. At the last minute, Annie popped through the dark-stained oak church doors with a bouquet of wild flowers in her grasp. She thrust them into Josephine's hands and placed a quick kiss on the woman's cheek. The glistening in Annie's eyes brought tears to Josephine's as well.

"It's time to go in," Quincy whispered, his hand gently touching the bride's elbow. "Your groom is waiting."

Groom? She caught her breath at the thought. What she'd thought impossible was actually happening. In a few moments she would be Samuel Pownell's wife. She giggled aloud at her afterthought—and Serenity Pownell's stepmother. She wished Serenity could be here.

Quincy looked at her curiously. She grinned up at him. "I'm ready."

The ceremony was simple; only Annie, Tad, Quincy, the pastor and his wife, Clare, and her faithful friends attended, but Josephine was delighted. Sam's eyes sparkled with love as he gazed down at his diminutive bride while the minister led them in their vows. Her voice caught on the phrase, "Till death do us part." She saddened at the sudden memory of Charity. Her heart whispered, *Please don't be sorry we're doing this, Samuel. Please don't be sorry.*

The warmth in his eyes assured her that he was as

committed to their vows as she. When the minister pronounced them husband and wife and whispered to Sam, "You may kiss the bride," Josephine's breath caught in her throat. For one short, tender moment their lips touched, a touch that held the promises of tomorrow, and tomorrow, and tomorrow.

As Sam straightened, he tucked her hand in the crook of his arm and turned toward their assembled friends. The newlyweds were blushing like schoolchildren after being caught sharing their first kiss. Josephine didn't begin breathing normally again until the minister introduced them as Mr. and Mrs. Samuel Pownell.

A big surprise followed the ceremony when Quincy Gatlin handed Sam a business envelope. "It's a reservation at the Bourbon Street Hotel. It's not a New York City establishment, but it's clean and respectable."

Josephine was surprised to see a cabriolet waiting for them as they emerged from church and into the late afternoon sunlight. "How? Where did that come from?" she asked, her hand firmly clasping her husband's.

He grinned at her, planting a kiss on the tip of her nose. "Earlier this afternoon, I sent Ed into town for it."

Mr. and Mrs. Pownell left the church in a flurry of joy and well-wishes from their friends. Josephine closed her eyes and leaned her head against the shoulder of her husband's smooth linen suit jacket and closed her eyes. The warm afternoon sun kissed her face. The wind rustled her curls. Despite the unbelievable happiness she felt, she remembered the day she married her first husband, Peter. *Till death do us part.* She saddened as she thought about her best friend, Charity, Sam's first wife. Who would have known, who could predict where God's plan would take her when she first came to Charity, a lost and frightened woman-child. To arrive at this point? *Almost unbelievable,* she thought. *So this is where it begins,* she prayed silently. *Where, dear God, will it end?*

The next morning, as the cabriolet bounced back up the road to Clare's home, Josephine was at peace with her thoughts of doom. *Whatever time we have together,* she mused, her eyes closed against the morning sun, *will be in my Father's hands, not mine.*

"Josephine? Josephine dear, what do you think?" She opened her eyes to find her new husband staring questioningly into her face.

"Huh? Oh, I'm sorry." A note of self-consciousness crept into her voice. "I didn't hear what you said?"

"I said I first considered moving to California, following the gold, but then I thought—all that sunshine? It can't be healthy! Besides, it brings out your freckles."

Josephine bolted upright. "What freckles?"

"This one . . . and this one . . . and this one. . . ." His lips touched each one.

She feigned indignation. "I don't have freckles, Mr. Pownell."

He gave a dramatic sigh and waved a hand in the air. "Whatever you say, my dear. Who am I to argue with the intrepid Mrs. Samuel Pownell?"

"You are incorrigible, Mr. Pownell. Now, what was it you were saying about California? Didn't we agree we were going to Missouri? Didn't you buy passage on the St. Louis-bound steamboat *Franklin* a few minutes ago?"

He broke into a broad smile. "Honey, I'm just teasing. Of course we're heading for Independence. You seemed so far away that I wanted to find out if you were listening to me."

She reddened. "I guess I was doing a little wool gathering, wasn't I?"

"You certainly were." He rolled his eyes skyward. "What were you thinking that took you so far from my side?"

"I was thinking about our marriage vows—the 'till death do us part' part."

He wrapped his arm around Josephine's shoulders and drew her to his side. "My dearest love, we only have today to love one another. Tomorrow and the rest of our future is in God's hands. It's up to us to fill today with as much joy as we can hold. Other than that we must claim the promise that God will never leave us or forsake us."

"You're right. I know you're right." Overwhelmed with emotion, she gazed up in his face. What a wonder it was having Sam by her side both physically and spiritually—a dream come true.

"Speaking of the future, I can't wait to see my beautiful daughter again. And I'm eager to show off my new wife to my darling Serenity. Imagine my little girl being a wife already herself. Incredible, isn't it?"

"Should we send her a telegram about our marriage?"

"I did that before you awakened this morning. Will it be a hardship to leave on Monday?" he asked.

"I do need to purchase fabric for a few lightweight dresses," she warned.

"Costing me money all ready."

"Costing you . . ." She swatted his arm with her reticule.

"I'm teasing. I'm teasing." He gave her an extra squeeze. "Seriously, your shopping will give me time to send the necessary papers to Willy Cox in Albany. He'll need to sell your place and liquidate whatever assets either of us might have. And I'll need to send instructions to Abe for bringing Dory and their son to Independence."

She looked at him sharply. "They do have a choice, don't they? What if their idea of the good life doesn't include Independence?"

A frown coursed his face as he considered her words. "I hope they'll want to come west. But if they don't, I'll instruct Willy to issue them a generous settlement, like I'll have him do for the rest of the staff."

Josephine gave him a satisfied pat on the knee. "How do you think Clare will take our leaving? She's pretty attached to you."

"Clare has known since the day she took me in that I would one day leave. She'll handle it just fine." The assurance in his voice didn't reassure her all that much.

Regarding Clare, Josephine proved to be right. The spinster had grown accustomed to having a family around to boss and to spoil.

In the days before Sam and Josephine boarded the paddleboat for Independence, Josephine caught Clare staring out of windows into nothing and swiping at tears that sprang uninvited in her eyes. The worst part was the growing fondness between her and Tad.

Set free from his life of fear, the child bubbled with joy and laughter. His keen mind could find humor in any situation. His love for music delighted everyone. Tad and Clare whiled away evenings at the pianoforte, she accompanying his flute. Music written by Beethoven, Mozart, and Bach filled the tiny cottage.

A few days before Sam, Josephine, Annie, and Tad were to leave, Clare came to the table with a proposition—leave Tad with her and she'd see he was educated in the best schools Europe had to offer and trained by the greatest of music teachers. "Tad is the most gifted child I have ever seen. He needs to develop his God-given potential," she argued in her no-nonsense schoolmarm tone.

There was no doubt that Tad had bonded with Clare more than anyone else in the household. Josephine knew that nothing would make the little boy happier than to stay with his beloved Aunt Clare. Josephine glanced across the platter of hotcakes at Sam. He arched an eyebrow. "He's yours, remember?"

"He's ours," she reminded him. "But we should ask Tad what he would like to do." Both knew what the child's answer would be without even asking.

"Are you sure?" Sam asked. Josephine nodded. Busy flipping pancakes, Clare missed the exchange between the newly married couple. "Clare, how would you ever afford to carry out the plans you've outlined?"

She cleared her throat, but remained with her back to them. "I have a little savings. And I could go back to work, teaching, maybe in Europe."

"I have a better idea," Sam began. "Since Tad is our responsibility legally, we pay you for his care and education."

Clare shook her head. "Oh, no, I couldn't allow you to—"

Sam chortled. "Allow us? Hardly. Even with the money Peter lost at the poker table, we will live just fine on what is left, I assure you."

For a moment the woman remained frozen, then the couple noticed her shoulders were shaking. They could hear her tears splattering on the hot griddle. Sam and Josephine looked at one another in surprise. The formidable Miss Clare Thornton was weeping.

"Samuel, this is so much more than I—" she sobbed.

Josephine helped herself to a dollop of marmalade for her hotcake, trying hard to hold her own emotions in check. "That's the deal. Take it or leave it. Of course, if you think the task would be too much for you—he is a small boy, you know."

Sam arose from the table, strode to the stove, and took the weeping woman into his arms. "Clare, you have done so much for me and risked so much for me, here is a chance to pass on your kindness to Tad. Don't deny us the pleasure out of some sense of false pride."

By the end of the week, Josephine had drawn up all the necessary documents to make Clare Tad's legal guardian and had arranged for a line of credit at the bank for the care and education of the boy genius.

"I never had anyone," Clare confided, "into whom I could pour all my energy. As a girl I was awkward and gawky. Papa said I was his ugly duckling and someday, I'd blossom into a beautiful swan." The woman blushed as she poured out her heart to Sam and Josephine on the night before they departed for Missouri. "Well, it never happened. The ugly duckling became a gawky goose. I decided that if I couldn't be lovely on the outside, I'd become lovely in the inside through God's grace."

Sam patted her hand tenderly. "You've certainly succeeded there."

"Tad is going to need all that loveliness of character God has developed in you," Josephine encouraged, "to make it in a world that is filled with hate for his kind—my kind, as well."

Clare beamed through a veil of tears. "I hope I don't let you down."

"You won't," Sam assured her.

~16~

Treasures of Love

JOSEPHINE'S WIDE-BRIMMED STRAW BONNET shaded her eyes against Missouri's blinding sun as she leaned over the railing of the Missouri River paddleboat, *Argot,* eager to catch a glimpse of the town of Independence, Missouri. Annie stood on her left, equally as eager to reach their destination. Even the sophisticated and urbane Samuel Pownell didn't try to hide his excitement upon reaching their new destination.

It had been a beautiful honeymoon trip up the Mississippi River from New Orleans for Sam and Josephine, but both were now eager to get on with their new life together. On board the *Argot,* Annie had made a new friend, a sixteen-year-old servant girl named Beth. Beth was traveling with her employer and his wife as well, except they were heading for California. Annie told Josephine that she was grateful she wasn't going any further than Independence. "I've had enough adventure to last me a lifetime," she confessed.

Excitement grew as the riverbanks showed more signs of life—human life. Josephine knew they couldn't be far from the city now. She jumped when the ship's bell sounded and the rhythmic splash of the paddles on the river slowed its cadence.

Up ahead, people swarmed the dock to greet the arriving paddleboat laden with family, pioneers heading west, goods from the big cities in the East, and food from the Southern plantations.

Josephine tugged at Sam's sleeve. "Do you see them? Do you see Serenity or Caleb?"

"There! There!" Annie shouted, dancing up and down with glee. "Beside the largest stack of wooden crates."

"I think you're right." Sam waved frantically. "Over here, Seri! Look over here!" he shouted.

The enormous paddleboat eased to a stop beside the wharf. The passengers waited impatiently for the ship hands to get the gangplank in place. As soon as the ship's steward gestured for the first passengers to disembark, the crowd surged forward.

Josephine knew the drill. They'd made numerous stops since departing in New Orleans. They'd changed riverboats at the mouth of the Missouri River.

The smartest move to make, she knew, would be no move at all until the majority of the people disembarked. Then she could exit the boat at her leisure. She knew this, but nothing could have kept her from pushing and shouting with the loudest of them. When she turned to see what Sam's reaction might be, she couldn't see him. He was way ahead of her. Not waiting to be told, Annie, too, charged down the gangplank.

With great effort, Josephine broke through the crowd to where Caleb and Serenity were waiting, only to find her husband already standing with his arm around his lovely daughter, grinning. "What took you so long?"

Serenity untangled her arms from Sam and hugged Josephine. "Welcome to Independence, Mama Pownell."

The two women giggled at the awkwardness of the term. In age, they were barely a decade apart.

After a round of kisses, hugs, and introductions, the men loaded the luggage onto the back of Caleb's wagon and Annie into the seat beside the driver, then climbed into the four-person carriage driven by Serenity's lawyer friend, Felix Bonner. In the rear seat, Serenity and Josephine talked incessantly throughout the ride home. And in the front seat of the carriage, Sam and Caleb did the same.

As the carriage rolled over the last knoll and Serenity's Inn came into view, Serenity leaned forward and pointed. "Welcome to Serenity's Inn. Isn't it beautiful? Don't you love it?"

Sam and Josephine tried to view the U-shaped sod structure as beautiful, but nothing in their past had prepared them for the reality of living in a mud house. Even the tulips growing along the front pathway couldn't ease the effect of seeing one's first sod house, especially one that housed your own kin.

Pasting on a game face, Sam asked, "You and Caleb did all this yourself?"

"Oh, no. The former owners built the main structure. They planned to open an Indian mission. The husband took sick and died, so the wife sold me the place and returned to her home in the East."

After a quick tour of the inn and Caleb's blacksmith shop, Serenity insisted Sam and Josephine change into more relaxed clothing before dinner. "You're in the Midwest now. The dress code is casual."

The oak paneled door to their bedroom had barely closed when Sam said, "I like that young friend of Caleb's.

I was hoping to find a law partner so as to give me more time with you. He might be the one to fill the bill."

"Moving pretty fast, aren't you, Mr. Pownell? You haven't been here for more than an hour and you're already planting roots." Josephine unlatched the lock on her trunk and opened the lid. Neatly folded gowns of cotton and wool brought a smile to her face. She lifted the top dress from the trunk and shook out the wrinkles. "I'm sure you'll want to give a lot of thought to a move of such importance."

Sam slipped his arms around her from the back and nibbled on her neck. "How did you become so wise?"

She leaned the back of her head against his chest and closed her eyes. "Marrying you was my first wise move." When she opened her eyes, her gaze rested on a bouquet of wild grasses tied together with a snippet of ribbon and hung on the wall beside the window.

"The kids have a great operation going here, don't you think?" She cast him a doe-eyed gaze. She'd been picking up slight nuances of his displeasure throughout the tour of the place. "I like the homey touches Serenity has put to the place—the gingham curtains in the great room, the lace doilies on the backs and arms of the sofa and upholstered chairs, the wreath of dried wild flowers over the mantle. There are so many. She truly loves her little home." She paused to give Sam an opportunity to respond. When he didn't, she continued, "Families traveling west must find this place a quiet haven of peace in the midst of the greatest turmoil of their lives."

"My, aren't you waxing eloquent?" he teased. Then in a serious note, he added, "And wasn't it convenient that they had no guests staying here when we arrived?"

Josephine chuckled as she turned so that Sam could

help her unbutton the back of her dress. "That's no accident, my dear. Serenity turned away two families after she received your second telegram from St. Louis regarding our estimated arrival time. They made room for us, but their season actually began last month. Seri was telling me how full they'd been since. The inn is definitely filling a need in this community." She wriggled out of her faille traveling dress, allowing the frock to slip to the floor. "For their business's sake, we need to find our own place as soon as possible."

"I agree." Sam removed a shirt from his portmanteau and shook out the wrinkles.

"Did you know that Seri and Caleb are planning on building a two-story clapboard inn with ten guest rooms? I was thinking I might enjoy being a silent partner in such a place. You said I should find an investment for my money."

"Now who's running ahead of herself. Maybe they won't want a meddling stepmother in their operation."

She shrugged. "Maybe—maybe not, I hadn't thought about the fact that I'm a stepmother now. Well, we'll have time to establish our boundaries with them now that we're here to live."

As she brushed the tangles out of her blond curls, Sam eyed the rough whitewashed mud and straw walls. "A regular house would be nice. I'm not too thrilled seeing my grandchildren born into—"

"Grandchildren? What do you know about grandchildren?" she chided. "Don't you say a single word about grandchildren until they're ready to tell us."

"Tell us? Tell us what?"

"About the baby."

"What baby?" he snorted.

"The baby Seri is carrying." She shot him a hopelessly silly grin. "Grandpa."

Sam's eyebrows narrowed. Bewilderment filled his face. "Grandpa? How do you know? Did Serenity say something about a baby?"

Josephine chuckled, running her hand gently along her husband's soft salt-and-pepper beard. "She didn't have to. Women notice these things."

"I don't believe it!" he scoffed, buttoning up his dark blue cotton shirt. "How can you tell?"

"Her coloring. The way she carries herself. The tranquil look in her eyes."

He shook his head. "She's as slim as a rail."

Josephine laughed as she pulled her hair into a bun at the nape of her neck. "Just like a man. She probably had a lot of morning sickness."

Sam pressed his hands against her shoulders. "And what do you know about morning sickness, my dear?"

Josephine lifted her nose and sniffed. "Women talk." Realizing he'd insulted her by bringing up the subject of her being childless, he drew her into his arms. She'd never discussed her concerns regarding children. But he never suspected that she was worried whether not she could conceive since she never had with her first husband.

"It's all right, honey. I'm sorry. We'll have us a whole house full of towheads like you."

She sniffed. "And if we can't, or I should say, I can't?"

"Then we'll fill our home with everyone else's children, all right?"

She wiped at a stray tear with her sleeve, then took one of his hands in hers and kissed it tenderly. "We'd better get out there. I can smell supper burning."

"Burning?" The man snapped alert. "Seri had better not be burning my supper!"

She helped him finish buttoning his shirt, then brushed past him to the closed door. "I don't know about you, but I'm starved!"

Sam laughed aloud as he tucked his shirt into his trousers and adjusted his suspenders on his shoulders. "You're always hungry, woman. For such a tiny package, you certainly can put it away."

Josephine ignored his remark and hurried down the short hallway to the great room. There, Annie and Serenity were setting the table. "Hi," Serenity said as she handed the silverware to Josephine and walked to the massive wood-burning cookstove on the far end of the room. "I spilled a ladle of soup when I was taste testing," she explained. "You can assure my father that I didn't burn his supper, no matter how bad it may smell in here."

"I don't know about that." Sam entered the room, his nose sniffing the air. "I remember a few smoky meals that you fed us back in New York."

Serenity jammed her hands on her hips and wrinkled her nose at her father. "No fair. I was learning then. I've had nine or ten months of experience since then. Besides, if you don't like my cooking, Caleb can show you where he keeps the chicken feed."

"Ooh!" Sam doubled over as if in pain. "That hurts, woman. I think I'll go see what Caleb's doing."

"He's milking Patty-cake," Serenity volunteered. "Josephine, there's a knife in the drawer and a fresh loaf of bread in the pantry if you want to make yourself useful."

"Absolutely," she responded. "I can see that there's no place for a prima donna in a prairie kitchen."

"That's for sure. I found that my female guests enjoy being in a kitchen once again, so I try to keep them busy while they're here. Besides, many hands make light work." Serenity laughed and ladled the hot stew into a large porcelain soup tureen. "Here, Annie, can you put this in the center of the table?"

With hot pads protecting her hands, Annie carried the tureen to the table.

"So, when did your in-laws leave for California?" Josephine asked as she deftly sliced through the freshly made bread.

"The beginning of March." Serenity brushed a lock of sweaty hair from her forehead. "Papa Cunard wanted to be certain they crossed the Sierras before the first hint of winter. I've missed Aunt Fay and dear Becca terribly since they left." She brightened and turned toward Josephine. "Have I told you how delighted we are to have you and Papa here?"

Josephine chuckled. "Oh, not more than fifty times in the last hour."

The door of the cabin swung open. Caleb strode in carrying several containers of preserved fruit, followed by Sam toting a bucket of fresh milk. "Just put the bucket on the counter over there." Caleb pointed to the rough hewn table against the wall.

The freshly oiled trestle table that occupied the center of the room groaned under the weight of all the delicious food Serenity was serving. Serenity beamed with delight. "Everything ready. Let's eat. Papa, why don't you sit next to, er, Mama Josephine right here. Calling Josephine "Mama" sounded strange to everyone assembled at the table. Serenity blushed, then continued. "Annie, you can sit across from them. Caleb and I will sit at each end."

As he seated himself on the bench beside his wife, Sam gazed at the mountain of food before him. "We're not going to eat all this in a month of Sundays."

"Speak for yourself, Sam," Josephine laughed. "I'm starved."

Serenity held out her hands, one to her father and the other to Annie. "In our family we join hands for the blessing," she explained.

With heads bowed, Caleb offered up a prayer of gratitude and praise. ". . . not only for the food, Lord, which You so generously provide, but for the safe arrival of Father and Mother Pownell and Annie. We humbly thank You for everything. Amen."

They'd barely finished the first course when Josephine broke into a grin. She glanced toward Sam, then back at Serenity. "Honey, we have a big surprise for you."

"You do?" Serenity shot a quick glance at Caleb.

"We do?" Sam eyed his wife questioningly.

"We do. Sam, maybe you should tell her," Josephine urged.

"Tell her what?" He looked bewildered.

"You know, about your change of heart . . ." Josephine rolled her eyes.

"Darling, I honestly have no idea what you are talking about."

Taking a deep sigh, Josephine announced, "Sam gave his life to Jesus a few months ago and has been baptized."

Serenity's jaw dropped open. Her spoon dropped into her soup bowl. Caleb gave a snort of surprise.

"Isn't it amazing? It took the Holy Spirit working through a dedicated spinster to do what neither Charity nor I could do. Couldn't you see the difference in him? I could." Josephine gushed while Sam reddened.

"Aw, come on, ladies, I wasn't that bad a scoundrel before, was I?"

Serenity hopped up from her chair and threw her arms around her father. "Oh, Daddy, my prayers have been answered. Every night and morning, Caleb and I lift you up to our heavenly Father. I love you so much. And I'm so happy for you, and for you, Josephine."

Throughout the rest of the meal, Serenity pumped her father for details on his exciting news. Sam told them about Clare Thornton's persistent reading of the Bible and of giving his heart to God at a revival meeting. "That one decision has made such a difference in my life."

Annie and Josephine helped Serenity clear the dinner plates from the table, then to serve the hot apple pie Serenity had made before leaving to meet the paddleboat.

Josephine took her first bite and rolled her eyes toward the ceiling. "Oh, Seri, you've got to teach me how to make a pie as good as this. Your crust is divine. Seri?"

Serenity hadn't heard Josephine's comment. She was staring intently at Caleb. "Should we tell them?" she whispered to her husband from the far end of the table.

"Tell us what?" Josephine asked, her eyes blinking with innocence.

Caleb shrugged his shoulders. "I don't know why not."

Serenity's eyes sparkled with delight as she reached out and took Josephine's hand and gazed at her father. "Daddy, guess what? Caleb and I are going to have a baby in September."

Josephine squealed, leaped to her feet, and hugged Serenity before Sam could respond.

"A baby?" Sam gasped and shot a quick look at his wife. "You were right. My baby is going to have a baby."

"I knew it. I knew it." Josephine hugged and rocked Serenity back and forth in excitement. "Oh, honey, we are so glad for you. Are you excited?"

Serenity nodded. "Most of the time."

"Oh! I can't believe it!" Josephine danced with joy. "I'm going to be married to a grandpa."

Everyone laughed at the look of consternation on Sam's face. "Hey, woman, I'm barely forty years old myself. And what about you? How will you like being a grandmother before your thirtieth birthday?"

Josephine paused, then broke into the warmest grin. Folding her arms as if cradling her grandchild, Josephine cooed, "I have bundles and bundles of love treasured in my heart for a little one. I'm going to be the best grandmother this baby could ever imagine."

"I feel so wealthy tonight." Sam blinked back a sudden flash of tears. "How rich can one man be? A loving wife, a beautiful daughter and son, and now, the prospects of a grandson."

"Or granddaughter," Josephine reminded.

Josephine watched Sam glance around the room. His eyes softened as they settled on Serenity's glowing face. She knew that it no longer mattered to her husband that the walls of Serenity's Inn were whitewashed sod and the braided rugs covered hardened mud.

Sam cleared his throat before he spoke. "Humans will go to any length to find their fortunes, to lay up treasures for themselves, and for what? If I've learned anything over the past year of living and growing, I've come to agree with the apostle Paul when he wrote, 'And the greatest of these is love.'"

also available from
THE SERENITY INN SERIES

Passion, love, and turmoil abound in the second volume of the Serenity Inn series. After receiving her inheritance, Serenity finds herself wondering if her friends sincerely accept her or are simply after her money. Coming of age, Serenity struggles with the issues of independence, true acceptance, and love. A novel filled with wonderfully interesting characters of the pre-Civil War era who welcome readers into their lives to experience the romance and adventure that can only happen at Serenity Inn.

0-8054-1674-9

available at fine bookstores everywhere